Beyond the Bend

OTHER BOOKS WRITTEN BY BARRY BLACKSTONE

Though None Go With Me

Rendezvous in Paris

Though One Go With Me

Scotland Journey

The Region Beyond

Enlarge My Coast

From Dan to Beersheba and Beyond

The Uttermost Part

Homestead Homilies

Rover: A Boy's Best Friend

North to Alaska and Back

Another Day in Nazareth

Sermonettes from the Seashore

Earth's Farthest Bounds

Angling Admonitions

Beyond the Bend

BARRY BLACKSTONE

RESOURCE *Publications* · Eugene, Oregon

BEYOND THE BEND

Resource Publications
An Imprint of Wipf and Stock Publishers
199 W. 8th Ave., Suite 3
Eugene, OR 97401

www.wipfandstock.com

PAPERBACK ISBN: 978-1-7252-9158-4
HARDCOVER ISBN: 978-1-7252-9156-0
EBOOK ISBN: 978-1-7252-9159-1

02/02/21

I saw your eyes open at birth. I watched them close in death. My face was the first you saw in life and the last you saw in death. While our journey together on earth is finished, your adventure in heaven has merely begun. Thank you, my son, for travelling your last roads with me. I penned these words so I will never forget the beginning and ending of our earthly pilgrimage together.

I would not have gotten this book project finished if not for the editing and compiling by my daughter and Scott's sister, Marnie. I would like to thank her for the numerous hours and many days she spent reading and correcting the errors in the original script, and the terrible emotions she had to endure reliving her brother's unexpected departure. Thanks again Marnie for all your labor; may you share in the eternal rewards of this book and the encouragement it will give other as they watch their loved ones pass 'beyond the bend'!

Contents

Prelude

The Challenge of Forty

I AM A NUMBERS guy. I hate mathematics, algebra, fractions, addition, subtraction, division, multiplication, trigonometry and algorithms. I hate all numbers connected with math, except one: statistics. I thrive on collecting statistics of anything in my life, whether the number of fish caught over my lifetime (9683), every sermon preached (15,156), days spent serving the Lord overseas (347), or Sunday school classes taught (1858). My bookshelves are lined with books of what some would deem worthless statistics recording aspects of my life.

I also love counting the number of days since my birth (24,050). I tell those who find this peculiar, that I have a Biblical mandate, "So teach us to number our days, that we may apply our hearts unto wisdom" (Psalm 90:12). Granted, I have expanded this precept to a myriad of life's accountings, but the Apostle Paul taught me, "So then every one of us shall give account of himself to God!" (Romans 14:12). I ask myself, "Could this include the numbers of my life?" My conclusion is a simple yes, and I have spent years doing just that!

The Word of God has a plethora of numbers found within its pages. The Apostle Paul wrote to Timothy, "All scripture is given by inspiration of God, and is profitable for doctrine, for reproof, for correction, for instruction in righteousness: that the man of God may be perfect, thoroughly furnished unto all good works." (2 Timothy 3:16–17). His use of the term "all" includes, not merely the content found among the pages, but the words as well, including numbers. In reading the inspired text, the reader will discover that certain numbers are used over and over again. Was God trying to tell us something in His inspired use of certain numbers?

The Biblical number that has fascinated me most over the years is the number forty. Through my study of the passages related to this number, I believe it to be a number indicating the testing of the Lord. The repetition of this number in Biblical stories relates to certain testing of the characters involved. Moses' life was divided up into three *forty* year divisions, each highlighting a different kind of testing (Acts 7:23, 30, 36). The first three kings of Israel reigned for *forty* years (Saul - Acts 13:21; David - 2 Samuel 5:4; Solomon - 1 Kings 11:42). The great high priest of Israel, Eli's judgeship lasted *forty* years (1 Samuel 4:18). Noah lived in the ark during the great flood which started with a rain storm that lasted *forty* days (Gen 7:4). Isaac and his son Esau were both *forty* when they took brides (Genesis 25:20, 26:34). The children of Israel wandered in the wilderness for *forty* years (Joshua 5:6). Moses first ascent to the top of Mount Sinai lasted *forty* days and *forty* nights (Exodus 24:18). The travels of the spies into the Promised Land lasted *forty* days (Numbers 13:25). Jonah preached to the Ninevites for *forty* days (Jonah 3:4). The children of Israel endured the taunting of the Philistine giant Goliath for *forty* days, before God sent a deliver through the shepherd boy from Bethlehem named David (1 Samuel 17:16)! Jesus was tempted *forty* days (Luke 4:2). Jesus stayed on earth *forty* days after His resurrection and before His ascension (Acts 1:3). I believe the number *forty*, and these specific examples, have relevance.

I wrote this book as a series of reflections regarding the events of my family that happened around this unique number *forty*. I will take you back to when I turned *forty*, the *fortieth* year of my ministry, and some other notable *forties* in my life. The heart of this book, however, will be the event that sparked this collection of remembrances - the death of my son, Scott, and a 5:00 a.m. phone call that set everything in motion on October 1, 2016 during Scott's fortieth year.

Introduction

The Life Of Scott Alexander Blackstone

IN ORDER TO SET the stage for the tragic events of October 1, 2016 to April 1, 2017, I want to share a little bit about Scott's life leading up to his final six months of life.

Scott Alexander (named after his grandfather Meister) Blackstone was born on November 7, 1977 at Concord General Hospital in New Hampshire at about one o'clock in the morning. Scott's parents, Barry and Coleen, were in their 4th year ministering at the Pembroke Bible Fellowship Church, an assembly they had started in the summer of 1973. Scott was three weeks late in his arrival, or at least according to those who set such times, but weighed in at just over seven pounds; healthy and happy. Coleen delivered Scott naturally with Scott's father having the privilege and honor of assisting the midwife in his birth. After being in the hospital all day and going through about eight hours of hard labor, Scott decided to come so quick the doctor on call had gone for a nap and by the time he arrived Scott was already out. He came into the world without a cry or a tear (he would leave the same way), and his father was the first to look into his bright blue eyes, followed by his mother (as it also was in the end). His father was the first to give him a bath; then he cried! He was a jaundice baby, and he would end his life jaundice because of the cancer that destroyed his liver. He was a complete joy as a baby and boy!

Scott wasn't even a year old when his parents moved him to Maine, their home state. In Aroostook County in Northern Maine, Scott first learned to walk and run and to fish; one of two life-long passions, the other was golfing! Scott would enjoy both to his late days (Actually the very last thing Scott and his father were able to do together was upon returning to Maine in November to go bass fishing one last time!). Living close to his grandparents (Stacy and Opal Meister of Washburn and Wendell and Phyllis Blackstone of Perham), Scott was able to experience family roots (Scott was buried on May 19, 2017 in the family burial plot at Fairview Cemetery in Perham, Maine on the bow of a hill on the Blackstone Road overlooking the ancestral homestead (1861) of the Blackstones; interestingly the same day his grandfather Blackstone was laid to rest; they had died seven weeks apart), and it was also in Northern Maine Scott lost a brother (Bevan Cherith) and got a sister, Marnie Lee. One of the early joys of Scott's life was the bond, friendship, and closeness he shared with his little sister; a relationship that only grew and matured throughout the rest of their lives together. This brother and sister also share the same spiritual birthday (October 30, 1983) the day the both of them gave their hearts to the Lord Jesus Christ after evening family devotions! Throughout the first 18 years of Scott's life he lived a carefree existence first in the small agricultural community of Westfield, Maine (his father pastoring the Calvary Baptist Church). It was here that Scott honed his fishing skills in a small pond near his home. Scott caught his first brook trout on May 15, 1982 at the tender age of 4 ½. By the age of 8 Scott was living on Moose Island (his father pastoring the Washington Street Baptist Church) off the coast of Maine! There Scott became quite the athlete in baseball (his Little League Team won the area championship in 1990 with Scott being the star player both as a pitcher (6–1, 2.50 era-including a no-hitter) and shortstop (a .652 average). After that Scott was on two consecutive junior high soccer teams that won the regional championship in both 1990 and 1991 (his teams were a combined 30–0 outscoring their opponents 134–33). When Scott was 14 his parents moved the family to the coastal city (his father pastoring the Emmanuel Baptist Church) of Ellsworth, Maine; just twenty miles from the world famous Acadia National Park. During Scott's high school basketball (his jersey number was 40-prophetic, but also the number his father used in his high school basketball career?) career for Temple Christian Academy he achieved a rare feat; scoring a thousand points. Actually Scott scored 1198 points (334 field goals, 200 foul shots, and 110 3-pointers) in his four year career (Scott averaged 28 points a game in his senior year including a 48-point, 21 rebound master piece on January 5, 1996), but it was during those years he also learned to play golf at the White Birches Golf Course, a sport that eventually would replace baseball, basketball, soccer, and for a time, fishing. His youthful love of fishing would return in his later years, but golf was his first love, playing it wherever he went eventually becoming a par golfer: without a handicap!

After high school Scott held down a variety of jobs, including working on a golf course and working at the local Wal-Mart. At the age of 29 Scott found his life's mission when he joined the United States Army. (It was the joy of his parents' lives to be at his swearing-in in Portland, Maine in 2006 and with him eight years later in Fairbanks, Alaska when he was honorably discharged from the regular Army!) Scott did his boot camp training at Fort Knox in Kentucky, and it was again his parents' honor to be there at Scott's graduation. Scott went on to do his heavy transportation training at Fort Leonard Wood in Missouri. After a short stay at Fort Benning in Georgia, Scott headed off to Fort Bragg in North Carolina, his home (Fayetteville) base for the bulk of his military career, and the place he would decide to call home after he got out of the regular army in 2014. Out of Fort Bragg, Scott's units (546th, 126th) would make three overseas deployments: 1) between July 24, 2007 and October 19, 2008 Scott made 25 combat supply missions (some of these missions out of Camp Airfjohn, Kuwait City, Kuwait lasted weeks) into all parts of Iraqi driving over 25,000 miles through enemy territory driving a gunship protecting the Iraqi convoys; 2) between October 22, 2010 and October 22, 2011 Scott completed 13 combat supply missions (again some of these IED lashed missions lasted a week or more) out of Camp Leatherneck, Afghanistan, in his last mission he was awarded the Purple Heart, 3) and between July 6, 2013 and April 1, 2014 Scott was again at Camp Airfjohn, Kuwait helping to pull equipment out of the Afghanistan War. Over Scott's eight years in the regular army, he received eleven medals and awards including the Combat Action Badge, the Iraqi and Afghanistan Campaign Medals, War on Terrorism Medal, Military Achievement Medal, Good Conduct Medal, Army Commendation Medal (Scott got this medal for actually saving an Afghani life), and the one he was most proud of: Drivers Badge (in six-years, traveling over 300,000 miles, he was accident free)!

After returning to civilian life, Scott joined the Army Reserves with the 650th Reserves Transportation Company out of Wilmington, North Carolina and started working for Coca Cola in the area around his adopted town of Fayetteville, North Carolina. By the end of 2015 Scott took advantage of the GI Bill and went back to school graduating from Heavy Equipment Academy in Seaport, New Hampshire in February of 2016. Returning to Fayetteville, Scott got his dream job working for Old Castle Lawn and Garden in one of their plants just outside Fayetteville running heavy equipment in their stockyard. With a good paying job Scott continued golfing and fishing, but by the summer of 2016 Scott had found another love: motorcycles. He bought his first Harley Davidson and enjoyed driving back and forth to work as well as taking long road trips on the weekend. In last September he bought his dream pickup: a big wheel, high-rider Ford F250 (he only got to drive it once) and was looking forward to a long and prosperous life, and then "Neuroendocrine Carcinoma" came to call.

Chapter 1

Departure Not Death

I KNOW YOU ARE thinking that Scott has died, not so, or at least not yet in the accounting of this the 40th year of his life; for in the midst of dealing with Scott's Neuroendocrine Carcinoma, his grandfather, in his 93rd year, departure for his home in glory. You will note that I used the word 'departure' not death. I have come to believe that the Biblical term for death for the Christian is departure, not death. I got this idea from the teachings of the Apostle Paul in II Timothy 4:6: "For I am now ready to be offered, and the time of my departure is at hand." My father was also ready for his departure to 'glory land'.

On Mother's Day 2014 Scott's grandfather Wendell had a massive heart attack while leaving the Perham Baptist Church. It hit so suddenly that Dad fell down the porch steps leading into the sanctuary and hit his head; most though he had died then. My wife and I were in Texas visiting Scott's sister Marnie at the time as they rushed Dad to the local hospital, and a phone call from my oldest sister Sylvia brought us home before Dad died, but he didn't die; it was not God's time (Revelation 1:18) of departure! Dad's recovery was nothing short of a miracle, but the fall at his heart attack caused a worse problem for him and the family: dementia. For thirty-three more agonizing, troubling months of life Dad struggled mentally resulting in his having to be put in the Veteran's (a World War Two vet of the Italian campaign-1944–1946) Home in Caribou, Maine because his wife Phyllis could no longer take care of him, also in her 90s. His stay there lasted 555 days, but on February 7, 2017 Dad was gloriously ushered into the presence of His Saviour; another truth I learned from the pen of Paul about believers: "We are confident, I say, and willing rather to be absent from the body, and to be present with the Lord." (II Corinthians 5:8) What a marvellous truth for every believer in the Lord Jesus Christ!

Ever since I started in the pastorate in 1973, I have dealt with the topic of 'departing saints'. This '. . .valley of the shadow of death. . .' (Psalms 23:4) has become a familiar path for me (my Dad's funeral was my 206th I would have my 207th within five days), but as I have said to the many that would listen to me, I have discovered that this 'valley' has many canyons and the canyon my wife and I are in now is far different than the others I have discovered in my travels through 'the valley of the shadow of death' with others! This one is personal, far more personal than any before including my father's. It might seem strange to you but I prayed for nearly three years for my Father's departure. I didn't have to watch him day in and day out like my mother, two sisters, and brother that live in Northern Maine. My rare visits were suffering enough to see the decline of a 'mighty man', in my opinion. In the end, my last visit just before Christmas 2016, I saw a broken man, a stranger to me, somebody I didn't even know. Such is the fate of dementia. I wanted my Dad to go home to Heaven for I know when I saw him again he would be the Dad I knew again, and God graciously answered that prayer.

That is why what is happening across the street (I am pecking (a two-finger typist) away at my laptop computer in my office of the Emmanuel Baptist Church across the street from the parsonage where Scott is resting) is different for me. For decades (ending 44 years in the pastorate) I tried to bring comfort to the grief stricken and now it is me grieving. I tried to bring consolation to the heavy-hearted and now it is me heavy-hearted. I tried to bring encouragement to the sorrowing and now it is me sorrowing. What I once only knew through observation I now know through experience. Only when you travel on the edge of the 'departure' of a son will you understand what Coleen and I are going through, but I am so thankful for that word 'through'. Peter said it best when he wrote in his first epistle that our trials (I Peter 1:6–7) are only for ". . .a season. . ." Actually, we have gone through autumn, and winter ends in just a few days. Can Scott make spring (he did), or will his departure be the greatest spring of his young life; to go to sleep in the drab of a worldly winter and awaken into a heavenly spring?

What Coleen and I are finding so difficult is the sensational ups (like a friend of our daughter, Matt Coffman, who flew Scott and Coleen home from Fayetteville, North Carolina to Trenton, Maine without cost!) and the spectacular downs (finding out your 39-year old son is dying of liver/lung cancer) that happen along the way to a 'departure'! For five months now we have been watching our beloved son dying. Some days we are excited, like yesterday, when we watch our son eat half of a Junior Big Max, something he hasn't done since this ordeal started in October last year. But two weeks ago today a doctor told us that Scott couldn't live through the coming weekend, and before we got him out of the hospital he fell and hit his head requiring eight stitches. A rollercoaster ride at best, the fears and disappointments seem to alternate between treatments, visits to the ER, and hospital stays. I know not the date (April 1, 2017) of my son's departure as I now know the date of his grandfather's departure, but it is my hope that this accounting will bolster the faith of someone who will have to travel down this same road behind my wife and me. I have also learned that we are not the first to travel through this 'valley'; others are ahead of us and praise the Lord they are looking back.

One of the great encouraging days of this journey came when the church phone rang unexpectedly. As I was sitting at my study desk preparing for a meeting, at first I didn't recognize the voice on the line, but soon heard the distinct voice of a former parishioner from my second church and a dear brother in Christ, Hershel Smith. Hershel had called to ask about Scott; Scott was just a kid when I pastored the Calvary Baptist Church of Westfield, Maine. After sharing our prayer requests for Scott, Hershel asked me to pray for his son Greg; it seems Greg was also dying (he would depart less than a week after that call) of "hardening of the heart." It was then I realized what different does it make if you are in your 60s and your son is in his 30s, or if you are in your 90s (Hershel is 94) and your son is in his 60s? Hershel and I have found ourselves travelling 'through the same valley' and what comfort and consolation that dear brother in Christ gave me that day. When two people are scarred by the same tragedy; what a marvellous rapport, what a miraculous communication, and what a comforting language we can have together!

What I feel strongly about is the fact that Jesus is the travelling companion of the departing. My son asked the Lord to be his Saviour on October 30, 1983. Since those early symptoms I believe Scott's Saviour was there knowing this was the time, the last great struggle of Scott's life, for Jesus promised to wander, to wade, and to walk through what John Newton called ". . .many dangers, toils, and snares. . ." No man, including my son, has ever walked through a more darksome valley than Jesus walked. No man, including my son, has ever suffered more grief than Jesus experienced. No man, including my son, has ever witnessed more sorrow than 'the man of sorrows'. If we know that He is there then even 'the valley of the shadow of death' can be a home to us for a while; a new normal for a season. Coleen and I have now joined the fraternity of the broken-hearted; we are now veterans of the war against cancer (we fought our first battle in 1997 against Scott's other grandfather's, Stacy Meister, lung/ liver cancer and our second battle in 2005 against Coleen's breast cancer). Departure is the ultimate victory!

Chapter 2

The Road of Life

MY FATHER WENDELL PREACHED the following sermon at Perham Baptist Church, in Perham, Maine many years before his death. I resurrected his evening sermonette and re-preached it at his funeral on February 19, 2017. My choice to add this message to a book primarily about my son speaks only of the similar roads of life my son and father shared. Both wore the title of ARMY veteran. Both gave their lives to the Lord as children. Both finished their roads of life with physical illness, despite one having many more years under their belt than the other. Both died the same year, just months apart from each other. Both are laid to rest beside each other in our family cemetery plot. For these reasons, I share my father's words.

"Mostly everyone here, at one time or another, has taken time to sit down and do some serious thinking. I believe if you were to ask any great man he would say he had done a lot of thinking over his life. We don't take enough time to stop and think during these busy days. I believe evidence of this is found in the reality of hell; for if people stopped to think if they were really going to hell, they would make a decision for Christ. Most people today are not thinking.

A story is told of a fellow in New York City who walked across the street and a car ran over him, killing him instantly. A crowd gathered around the victim, and somebody said, 'What was this guy thinking?" Someone else responded, "He wasn't thinking at all! That's why he got run over!' One more story and we will get to our lesson for the evening. Sam Jones, a simple, country, Methodist, circuit-riding preacher, went to hear a man by the name of Peter Richardson speak. Richardson had a unique personality and was well-known for his great preaching. Sam sat there listening intently to the preacher. Sam's face lit up and looked away as if he were thinking. At the conclusion of the sermon, Sam was overheard saying, 'I have learned today that a pulpit is not a prison, but a throne. I have learned that the preacher is not a prisoner, but a king with the scepter of the Scriptures in his hand as he sits on a throne of power!'

Most everyone in attendance today has made a decision to follow Jesus and is on the road of life. In 1944, I had the opportunity to serve in the ARMY, where they stationed me in the mountains near the Yugoslavia border. Serving as a medic, I had a great deal of time to think. I decided I had to live someplace, and I had better learn how to live anywhere. Having been a Christian for only a short time, I used my extra time to start reading my Bible. Now I haven't lived up to all that is found in the Bible, but I have tried. Remember: Christians are not made in a day, but through years of right living and thinking (Philippians 4:8)! Today I want to speak on Hebrews 12:1–2, which reads, 'Therefore, since we are surrounded by such a great cloud of witnesses, let us throw off everything that hinders and the sin that so easily entangles. And let us run with perseverance the race marked out for us, fixing our eyes on Jesus, the pioneer and Perfecter of faith. For the joy set before him he endured the cross, scorning its shame, and sat down at the right hand of the throne of God.' As we read in verse one, we have a great cloud of witnesses surrounding us. I believe this 'cloud of witnesses' refers back to chapter eleven, the faith chapter. These men and women are referred to as heroes or champions of the faith. Abel offered a better sacrifice to God than Cain, through which he obtained the testimony that he was righteous. God took Enoch to heaven because he was pleasing God. Noah prepared an ark for the salvation of his household and became an heir of righteousness. Abraham, when he was tested, offered his only son Isaac. These are but a few of the great men who put their trust in God and endured to the end. They challenge us with their faith. Can we stay on the road of life and endure to the end like them?

We have older people in our group who are witnesses to our actions. I admire the older people of this church for their testimony and faithfulness. They have been a great help to me on my road of life. The last part of verse one says, 'Let us run with perseverance the race that is set before us.' We each have a road to run during our life, whether broad, narrow, smooth or rough. Matthew 7:13–14 says, 'Enter ye in at the strait gate for wide is the gate and broad is the way that leadeth to destruction and many there be which go thereat. Because strait is the gate and narrow is the way which leadeth unto life and few there be that find it.' How true this is today, with busy streets, but few walk the Church steps! It says: s-t-r-a-i-t, not s-t-r-a-i-g-h-t. Now the word strait means 'hard'. Anything that is worth doing is hard work. It is hard to get on the right road and stay on the right road. It is never hard to do wrong. Even dead fish go down stream, but it takes live ones to go up stream.

In a physical race, we prepare by running distances each day, eating the right foods, getting enough sleep, and so on. I believe it is the same with our spiritual race. We need plenty of Bible reading and study, prayer and supplication and keeping busy in the Lord's own work. 1 Corinthians 9:24–25 says, 'Know ye not that they which run in a race run all, but one receiveth the prize? So run that ye may obtain, and every one that striveth for the mastery is temperate in all things. Now they do it to obtain a corruptible crown, but we an incorruptible.' Hebrews 12:1 reads, 'Let us lay aside every weight and the sin which doth so easily beset us.' I could never get over why the word weight is put before sin. I believe sometimes we have weights that bother us more than sins. Many people carry weights that are not actual sins, such as ignorance. While it is not a sin to be ignorant, it is a sin to stay ignorant concerning the Bible. Weights and sins can go hand in hand; what if I go down the street with a cigarette in my mouth and a grindstone under my arm? Smoking (probably the cause of my son's cancer; a practice he indulged in during his twenties, gave up, but took up again just before his death) is a dirty habit that becomes a sin oftentimes, so I should throw the cigarette away. There is nothing basically wrong with a grindstone, but it could be a fault, it could hinder me from performing a duty. A fault is something that holds me down, or holds me up, or holds me back! Holding on to it at the wrong time could be as dangerous (cancer sick dangerous) for me as a sin. Weights can and often turn into sins. Anything which holds us back from doing God's best should be put away. Romans 13:12 says: 'The night is far spent, the day is at hand. Let us therefore cast off the works of darkness and let us put on the armour of light.'

At the end of the road of life the Bible tells us in Hebrews 12:2, 'Looking unto Jesus the author and finisher of our faith who for the joy that was set before Him endured the cross, despising the shame, and is set down at the right hand of the throne of God.' Jesus did this all for us. Hebrews 2:9 reads, 'But we see Jesus who was made a little lower than the angels for the suffering of death, crowned with glory and honor that He by the grace of God should taste death for every man.' And Philippians 2:8 reads, 'And being found in fashion as a man He humbled Himself and became obedient unto death, even the death of the Cross.' Who could possible travel the road of life without this One? So let us take the challenge of Hebrews 13:13, 'Let us go forth therefore unto Him without the camp bearing His reproach.'" Thanks Dad: still walking the Road!

Chapter 3

Turning Forty

ON MARCH 6, 1991, I wrote the following for my fortieth birthday:

"I turned forty today! For a guy who never thought he would reach twenty, I feel like quite an old fellow. As I reminisce about this birthday, my mind slips back to thirty years ago when my sister and I waited for a small yellow bus by the roadside on our family's homestead in Perham, Maine. Our trip to the four room country schoolhouse was more of a journey than a ride, and on this fortieth birthday of mine, I rode that yellow bus all over again. I retraced that old bus route and found recollections enshrined in the temple of my memory bank. Sylvia and I climbed the black, dusty steps and took our seats on the cracked leather. We made our way down the hill and across the Salmon Brook as we headed toward the Tangle Ridge Road. With each stop, the bus filled with neighbors and good friends. As the yellow bus drove around each corner of the woods around the Tangle Ridge Road, I lingered in the memories of those gentler and simpler days when conversations were clean and kids were kind (don't remember one bully). After an hour of weaving through the Perham roads, we reached our destination, the Perham Elementary School, ready for a day of math with our teacher, and a game of recess basketball. Our classrooms moved counterclockwise, as you graduated from one grade to the next, climbing the ladder of achievement. We spent our first two years with Mrs. Conroy, and then off to Mrs. Beverage's third and fourth grade class. Those first four years on the left side of the hall laid the groundwork for crossing the hall to Mr. Humphrey and Mr. Harper's rooms. By the end of Mr. Harper's eighth grade, we had gone as far as Perham Elementary School could take us. We respected our teachers and their instruction in our lives. Our free hour at noon recess was spent playing basketball, not sneaking a smoke. We learned reading, writing and arithmetic, with history, geography and spelling explained. SATs and Colorado placement tests never loomed. We grew and learned in a wholesome place with ordinary people as our guides. This red, two room, four teacher school house has long since burned and been remodeled into an apartment building, and now that building has burnt down and has been replaced with a residential trailer. Decades have passed, yet, for me it remains my country school, the Perham Pirates, eight grades of country kids who didn't have much, know much or want much."

Oftentimes life seems like my little rural school, doesn't it? We start in the elementary room learning the basics of life: walking, talking, and growing. We move to the next level where we discover our new abilities allow us to run, explore and find friendships. By the time we cross the hall into adolescence, we have matured enough to make vital decisions, although some might still be a tad ridiculous. We spend our teenage years experimenting, and for some those experiments come at a cost. Young adulthood finds us making the most important decisions of our life: career, relationships, and pursuits. Some make logical and reasonable choices, but others make choices that will haunt them for the rest of their lives, even if that life is short. As I ponder the last days of my dear son, I am confronted with a perplexing question: Do the choices we make at twenty affect the life we have at forty? Can we find a direct coordination between the two?

When I turned forty I was just finishing up a five year pastorate in my third church (Washington Street Baptist Church of Eastport, Maine). I had been married for 18 years and had two children: Scott was 14 and Marnie was 12. I had lived a healthy lifestyle and I was ready to accept a new pastorate that would prove to be my church of a lifetime (29 years at this printing)! I was set to fulfill the dream of a long-term pastorate, and maybe my last.

Contrast that with my son who at the beginning of his 40th year was fighting for life itself. My wife and I found our Scott's strange ailments began in September, 2016. On October first an Emergency Room doctor gave him the cancer diagnosis. Within two months his body is retaining fluids, has lost 20 pounds, can no longer stand due to pain; his liver is painful to the point he can no longer stand the discomfort, he is aging rapidly to the point where he didn't even look like himself, and he can hardly walk. This is how my wife and I found our 39 years old son when after an 18-hour drive from Maine we arrived at the Cape Fear Hospital in Fayetteville, North Carolina.

I believe that all disease originated with the entrance of sin into the world (Genesis 3). It is also my belief that some diseases bear more of a resemblance to sin than others, and cancer is top on the list. I have come to believe the Biblical word is 'canker', a consumption or gangrene. Paul uses the word to describe the speech of Hymenaeus and Philetus in 2 Timothy 2:17 saying, ". . .and their talk will spread like gangrene."

When I first saw my son after an eight month separation, I knew my boy was being consumed by something. When I learned that thing to be cancer, like gangrene, was eating up his inside, I could only imagine the diabolical ingenuity of the Devil in his assault on the human body. Like Job, I believe Satan had to get permission (Job 2:4–6) to attack my son. The cancer my son has, however, is like the sin that created it—aggressive, uncanny, and seemingly unstoppable. Paul accurately writes, "For we wrestle not against flesh and blood, but against. . .spiritual wickedness. . ." (Ephesians 6:12). Some maladies bear the mark of the wicked one. What I have seen of Scott's cancer, Satan's vile paws are all over it!

The day I turned forty I dreamt of good dreams. I was living a blessed life with my wife, son and daughter in the service of my King. All was right with my world. Yet, for my son, his fortieth would look so different. I could have never dreamed that before my son's fortieth birthday he would have to face one of life's greatest struggles: a raging cancer consuming his flesh ounce by ounce, pound by pound, breath by breath, step by step, and thought by thought. Scott's schooling is about over and I can see that the Good Lord left for him the hardest course of them all.

Chapter 4

Humming a Tune

AT THE HEIGHT OF my son Scott's battle with cancer, my father's health continues to decline as well. His departure from this life to his eternal home will soon be here. Over the years, I have written scores of articles on my Dad's life. When I turned forty, I penned these words about him:

"Forty years have passed and the picture I have of my Dad has now become much clearer. I remember my Dad as a demonstrator, not a dictator; a quiet man who spoke little, but taught much. Only in these latter years have I come to realize how much his teachings and example have shaped my life.

Dad taught me how to work by working. From before sunrise until after sunset, seven days a week and with few vacations, he worked our family's dairy and potato farm in Perham, Maine. Through seasons of plenty and want, Dad maintained a heritage passed on to him from his father, and in turn he passed on to his son, Jay. As I ponder my father's example of labor, I ask myself, is this why I work in the church as he did on the farm? Is his example why I dislike being away on a Sunday or any other time the flock needs to be fed? Is his example why I am content just to plant and sow, to feed and provide, to harvest and reap? Is his example why I desire to pass on my spiritual heritage to another generation?

Dad taught me how to pray by praying. A meal never passed without him bowing his head in prayer, whether potato house or farmhouse. A night never passed without him kneeling by his bed in prayer beside my mother. A Wednesday night never passed, whether planting or harvesting, that you could not find him attending prayer meeting at his church. Is his example why I am confused why Christians choose not to find time to pray? Is his example why I believe prayer to be one of the most essential virtues in the Christian Faith?

Dad taught me how to be present by being present. Dad was there when my dog Rover was hit by a passing car, and somehow made everything better. Dad was there when I lost my only tournament basketball game at the Bangor Auditorium, and he said the right thing, "It's only a game." Dad was there when I called with financial trouble, and offered the right advice and a helpful check. Dad was there when I struggled with my calling to return to my home church as their pastor. His support never wavered, despite the churches rejection of me. Is his example why I desire to be present when others are in need? Is his example why I drop everything when someone calls no matter the time or trouble?

My father's example would influence me in ways I failed to recognize until decades passed. My father's demonstrations, not dictations, helped shape me into the image of our Saviour, the Lord Jesus Christ (Rom 8:29). I see clearly now my Dad as a pastor, and I, his congregation."

At my Dad's funeral, I decided to share one aspect of Dad's life that remains so helpful to me:

"As we gather this day to ponder Dad's life, I pause and reflect. To someone here, he was husband. To others, he was a father, grandfather, and friend. To pick one memory to share today would be impossible. The memories remain too numerous to speak of his legacy to us. I could talk of his strength, as I can count on one hand the times I saw my father cry. I could talk about his love of hunting and fishing. If you ever eat his venison and trout, you know they would melt in your mouth. I could speak of his resounding faith and unashamed witness, but close your eyes and remember when Dad was at his best. Whether milking the cows in the morning or digging potatoes in the afternoon, he never complained about the work still to be done. You could always find Dad humming a tune! Many books have been written on how to live a long and full life. Could there be one simple detail the wisest of scholars have overlooked? Perhaps, it is a simple as humming a tune and keeping a song in your heart. Ask Dad his plan for years of keeping a good health and he would answer, 'a good nap!' But, I am here to tell you what we have known all along and what Dad has long since given us a clue. We must follow Dad's example and work through each day and labour while humming a tune!"

We concluded Dad's funeral with a Christmas recording of Dad singing Ron Hamilton's wonderful song, "Rejoice in the Lord." I believe Dad taught us all how to sing. But, the best thing he taught us was the precept of

Paul found in his letter to the Ephesians, "Speaking to yourselves in psalms and hymns and spiritual songs, singing and making melody in your hearts to the Lord" (Ephesians 5:19). I have come to believe my Dad's example of humming a spiritual tune has given me a wonderful source of comfort during these difficult days. When I am most discouraged, I find myself singing a favorite church hymn. Humming a hymn is beautiful therapy. I am grateful for this comforting technique taught to me by my Dad, as we face the dark days of cancer with my son.

Chapter 5

A Letter to My Parents

I TOOK TIME ON my fortieth birthday to write this letter to my parents, the two most influential and supportive people in my life. I am so grateful to still have my mother's support as I watch my son battle this dark lonesome valley of cancer. Here is my letter to them:

"Dear Mum and Dad,

People often write of the things their parents did for them during their lives. I, however, desire to thank you for what you chose *not* to do in my life. While fifty percent of all marriages end in divorce before their children reach forty, I am mindful your marriage remains. (My Mum and Dad were married sixty-seven years at my Dad's death.) While most parents abandon their children at some time during their lives, I am mindful you never did. Statistics show that three quarters of families resort to drugs to cope with difficult times. I am mindful, you never did. While most parents resort to cursing at their children when aggravated and frustrated, I am mindful you never chose those words for your children. While most parents spend their money on gambling or other forms of selfish pleasure, I am mindful you wisely spent your money. While most parents try pawning off their parental responsibilities to others, I am mindful you chose to raise us yourselves. While most parents send their children to church alone for others to tell them about God, you were the first to tell us of our Savior. While most parents take little interest in the well-being and outcome of their children's lives, I am mindful you didn't.

Do you remember these moments? When I split open my head after you had told me to be careful chasing my sister, I thought you would royally scold me, but you didn't. When I had to stay in the hospital after surgery on my neck, I thought you would leave me there alone, but you didn't. When I woke up one morning and couldn't walk, I thought you would still make me go to school, but you didn't. When I fouled out of my last high school basketball game at the Bangor Auditorium, I thought you would really be hard on me, but you didn't. When I wanted to be a summer missionary to Australia instead of helping out on the farm, I thought you would say no, but you didn't. When I told you I would take Coleen as my wife, I thought you would put up a fight, but you didn't. When I called and told you that I thought the Lord was calling me to start a new church in New Hampshire, I thought you would give me a million reasons why I should never go, but you didn't. When I phoned from New Hampshire with tax problems, I thought would tell me it was my own problem, but you didn't. When I decided to return to Maine after five years in New Hampshire, I thought you would say, "I told you so," but you didn't. When I visited you telling you I believed the Lord was leading me to pastor our home church, I thought would say I was crazy, but you didn't.

Thank you Mum and Dad for never doing any of these things; I am who I am today because of your choices. I love you both."

I have been blessed my entire life with grand, kind, helpful and gracious parents. Despite my Dad's departure from this earth and mother's declining health, I am grateful the Good Lord allowed my parents to be with me during this test of watching my son die. It is difficult losing a son. No parent should have to bury their son. I started writing this book on some of the darkest and most difficult days of my life. To date I have sat in the hospital, cancer clinic or ER for thirty-six days and 240 hours of the 154 days since Scott's diagnosis. I like what Vance Havner once wrote, *"Sitting for weeks in a hospital is enough to make a well man sick!"* As my son loses weight (60 pounds to date), I have also lost (15 pounds to date) weight and am troubled with my right kidney, likely a stone of which I am prone. As I sit with him, I think of all our plans that now lie in shambles. Scott's twenties were difficult years in the choices he made, which weakened our own relationship. His thirties found him serving in the military and deployed three times and living in Alaska for his fourth duty station. Our times together in twenty years became rare. But shortly into 2014, Scott came home more. We began fishing together again and started to dream about distant fishing holes we wanted to explore. Since this tragedy of cancer, I feel as Jacob said when he thought he had lost his beloved son Joseph, ". . .all these things are against me" (Gen 42:36). But, I have also laid claim to the promise, "Commit thy ways unto the Lord; trust also in Him; and He shall bring it to pass" (Ps 37:5); this recipe of commitment, trust and promise have been my answer during this trial.

I believe there is nothing left to chance with God. My God is never taken by surprise. While Scott's cancer diagnosis shocked my daughter Marnie and proved a numbing revelation to my wife and me, the Lord remained steady. One of the attributes of God that has helped me understand Him in so many situations and circumstances like this is His 'foreknowledge.' God knew this trial would be part of His divine plan for Scott and us.

Many have asked, "How are you coping under this circumstance?" I believe we are not to be *under,* but *above* it. By God's grace we have travelled through six months. Every twist and turn navigated by God's mercy and grace. Ours is the grace Paul talked about: grace not merely of sunny days, birds singing and a bright blue sky, but a grace born of adversity, agony, and ache. Paul writes, "And He said unto me, my grace is *sufficient* for thee: for my strength is made perfect in weakness. Therefore will I rather glory in my infirmities that the power of Christ may rest upon me! Therefore I take pleasure in infirmities (cancer), in reproaches, in necessities, in persecutions, in distresses (watching a son dying) for Christ's sake: for when I am weak, then I am strong!" (2 Corinthians 12:9–10)

Where did I learn to refocus on the message and instruction of the Word of God? The answer is simple: my parents. I remain grateful they made the hard choices for my siblings and me. Their love and dedication to the Lord and each other laid a foundation in the Lord for which I could never repay them.

Chapter 6

Simply Trusting

THE MYRIAD OF LETTERS, cards and calls wishing us the best over the last six months are too many to count. Accompanying those notes have been sayings, poems and prose to help us endure this heavy-laden ordeal. One of the best came just a few days ago from my oldest sister Sylvia, in which she shared the words to an old church hymn. My sister has spent her lifetime playing hymns, psalms, and spiritual songs (Colossians 3:16). While she spent half her life as an English teacher in the public school system, the other half she dedicated to being a sacred musician.

In her letter, she penned the words of Edgar Page Stites hymn, "Simply Trusting." Stites, born in 1836, served as a faithful member of the Methodist Church in Cape May, New Jersey. A veteran of the Civil War, Edgar spent the bulk of his life as a riverboat captain, while later becoming a missionary in the Dakotas. His other famous hymns include, "Beulah Land." Dwight L. Moody found his poem "Trusting Jesus" in an 1876 newspaper, and upon reading it gave it to his associate Ira Sankey. Sankey turned the poem into the familiar melody we sing today.

There is little doubt as to why my dear sister sent me the following words:

> Simply trusting every day, trusting *through a stormy way*;
> Even when my faith is small, trusting Jesus-that is all.
> Brightly does His Spirit shine into *this poor heart of mine*;
> While He leads I cannot fall, trusting Jesus that is all.
> Singing if my way is clear, *praying if the path be drear*;

If in danger, for Him call, trusting Jesus-that is all.
Trusting as the moments fly, trusting as the days go by;
Trusting him whatever befall, trusting Jesus-that is all.

The Bible teaches us to not be anxious no matter the trouble, including my son's sickness. Fear, fretting and fussing must be replaced by believing and trusting. In seasons like this, it is easy to doubt and debate, rather than trusting my Guide. I, like Job, have learned to say, "'The Lord gave, and the Lord hath taken away; blessed be the name of the Lord" (Job 1:21). I also conclude, like Job, "What? Shall we receive well at the hand of God, and shall we not receive evil?" (Job 2:10).

The words that fell from my wife's mouth upon her own diagnosis of cancer still ring in my mind, "Why *not* me?" Why not Scott? Why not us? Years of praying for the illnesses of other's children, so, why not Scott, why not us! The true test of one's trust comes not by reading, talking, praying or even singing about it. Trust comes when it is tested and tried and lived.

Please hear me. I am no super saint. I collapse into tears. I am angry. My feelings are all over the map given any moment. There are hours I desire to throw in the towel and not walk by faith. Trust, however, grows by exercise. There seems to be this popular misconception that when we become a Christian all the characteristics of Christ come with the Spirit. The Spirit does contain these virtues (Galatians 5:22–23), but they must be cultivated. Trust grows when challenged. The stress and strain of tests of faith can cause weariness and weakness, our trust in the Lord wobbles. In these moments, we must collapse into the arms of a loving Father, who promises to strengthen us.

Jesus taught us that our faith need only be the size of a mustard seed in order to be effective. With this guide, we press on each day, assured our loving Heavenly Father will provide. Peter teaches, "Casting all your care upon Him; for he careth for you" (I Peter 5:7). Whether the "care" is a dying child, funds to pay for medical needs, a heartbroken spouse, newly widowed mother, Peter's promise contains the word "all!" New obstacles arise at any moment of any day. Unseen difficulties arise. For these reasons, we must simply trust and believe the Lord to guide us through with minimal doubt or worry. The mustard seed can and will move the mountain if we are doubtless. There were moments in North Carolina when I thought we would never get Scott to Maine. There were moments in December I thought we would never see the New Year. There are even moments now I wonder if we will reach spring, yet we are still here. My son remains home where he wants to be. My wife cares faithfully for our son and her ninety-two year old mother.

My prayer, as we reach the end, is that we will not waver in our trust. According to John, faith overcomes the world (I John 5:4). I am confident my son will be delivered from this dreaded disease, whether a miraculous deliver or departure to a land that is cancer-free. Vance Havner wrote a book during the passing of his wife Sarah from "Cushing" disease. He entitled it, "Though I Walk Through The Valley." He wrote of simple trust as being *"shipwrecked on God and stranded on Omnipotence."* This is where my wife and I find ourselves. Shipwrecked on God; stranded on the Omnipotence and safe in the arms of Jesus. May it be said of us, as it was of Job, "In all this Job sinned not" (Job 1:22).

Chapter 7

A Yesterday at Forty

THERE IS A PLETHORA of time to think back on life, when you are caring for a sickly lad. As I write today, Scott receives his first visit from a Hospice nurse. I desire to escape the reality of this day and all that Hospice indicates. I find my mind wandering to days gone by, as I dread all the tomorrows to come.

As Scott fights through his fortieth year, I want certain things of yesterday to be remembered tomorrow. I wrote a few stories on my fortieth birthday in 1991. Here is one, I don't want to forget:

"Solitary strolls into the stories of my past remain as much a part of my life now as meat and potato suppers. Too often I ramble through the last four decades without purpose or plan in writing my memories down. My only goal was but to capture the recollections of my family and friends in black and white, so others might know what makes me, me. I purposed each week, to break away from my life as a country pastor and turn back time to my boyhood in a barnyard in Northern Maine. With my imaginary walking stick in hand, I travel back to the places and the people that made up that colorful part of my life. I walk again down old pasture trails that lead to wonderful times of nostalgic nuggets from my family's history.

Since I started this writing project I have learned so much about my roots. I met Sophronia (a great-great-great grandmother) and a sheep dog turned cow dog named Lady. I met my grandfather's work horses Dolly, Bob and Champ. I learned a Blackstone gravestone was the first ever to be laid in the Fairview cemetery of Perham, Maine. I learned my great-great grandmother Amelia was the first school teacher Perham ever hired. I learned my family uncovered skeletons from an old cemetery when they dug the cellar of our new potato house in 1930. Every turn of the path I discovered a new piece of the puzzle of my life.

My pace seems to quicken as I merrily skip through these memories. Each time I find myself in yesterday I uncover a world all but lost now. The pandemonium of progress has invaded my homestead today, but yesterday it is just as I left it; the Holsteins are still grazing in the pasture. My dog Rover is still chasing cats in the barnyard; the old John Deere tractor is still plowing the Paul Place. There is still "milking time" and "digging time." Gramp Blackstone is still in his garden weeding, and the homestead is still a potato/dairy farm. It is all just like it used to be.

When I close the door of my present in order to open the door to my past, I withdraw to a yesterday unaffected by today. I know I cannot remain there. However, for the blessed intervals I do, I return renewed and recharged. What a few short visits into yesterday have done for this farm boy caught in a city at forty fighting a life-ending illness!"

Could God have given us the capacity for mediation, so that in times of deepest grief we can escape to better times? I like what the old preacher once said while commenting on II Corinthians 12:9–10, *"Lord, you have the strength and I have the weakness-let's team up!"* Just before writing this chapter, I watched a nearly two hour video of my father's funeral, which included a twenty minute picture and song tribute compiled by my niece Kristen. What memories those pictures brought back! The meditation was sweet, and a break from what is going on across the street at my home. Many like to use the term "lost," when referring to someone who has passed away. But, I have not lost my dad, and I will not lose my son. You cannot lose anything that you know right where it is, and I know right where my father is and where my son is going!

Another aspect of mediation clearly seen in Scripture and applicable to my family's situation, is the comfort that comes while meditating on the word of God. Psalms 1:3 reads, "But his delight is in the law of the Lord; and in his law doth he meditate day and night." God also challenged Joshua with these words, "This book of the law shall not depart out of thy mouth; but thou shalt meditate therein day and night, that thou mayest observe to do according to all that is written therein: for then thou shalt make thy way prosperous, and then thou shalt have good success" (Joshua 1:8). How can one even imagine prosperity and success while battling cancer? I have come to believe it is only possible when you think of what shall be. For the Christian, we not only have the past to lighten our way, but we have the blessed hope of the future to brighten our day. Paul wrote, "But it is written, Eye hath not seen, nor ear heard, neither have entered into the heart of man, the things which God hath prepared for them that love him." (I Corinthians 2:9–10). All I see currently is my beloved son wasting away to nothing. Yesterday we weighted Scott as we have done every two weeks for the last three months in order to keep an eye on his strength. He is down to 128 pounds from 189 pounds when this ordeal started. Needless to say he is 'skin and bones' now. This is what my eyes see, skin and bones. Over time Scott's voice has declined in volume and his speech is a tad confused. What we hear is not comforting or hopeful.

But, there is a day coming when Scott will be in his glorified body and what we see and hear will be wondrous. Paul writes, "According to my earnest expectation and my hope, that in nothing I shall be ashamed, but that with all boldness, as always, so now also Christ shall be magnified in my body, whether it be by life, or by death. . . . .For our conversation is in heaven' from whence also we look for the Saviour, the Lord Jesus Christ: who shall change our vile body (there is nothing more vile than a body ravaged by cancer), that it may be fashioned like unto His glorious body, according to the working whereby He is able even to subdue all things unto Himself" (Philippians 1:20, 2:20–21). I believe even in the midst of such misery we can have "a foretaste of glory divine" and the heavenly power that will change us (I Corinthians 15:52–54). Today, my dad is walking on golden streets and eating celestial food. In the not too distant future, my father will share his meal with my son.

I believe in these promises (II Peter 1:4), for they are not just words on my walls or sayings on my lips. They are checks of God that will one day be cashed in at the bank of heaven. I have a checking account up there (Matthew 6:19–21). I am using the checkbook of faith to draw on those heavenly accounts for my needs here and now. Meditation is the means we can use, whether from the past or the future. On this day I am resting in the power of "another" (Matthew 11:29–30). I am like the man who once said, "I've wrecked my constitution and am living on my bylaws!" The doctors have done all they can do. Now, I entrust my son into the hands of the Great Physician!

Chapter 8

Angels Unaware

SHORTLY BEFORE MY SON Scott turned thirty-nine, I preached a sermon on Hebrews 13:2 which reads, "Be not forgetful to entertain strangers: for thereby some have entertained *angels unawares*." Over the course of my life there have been a few 'angelic' encounters, however, none as many as when my wife and I received the news of our son's debilitating cancer diagnosis.

Over the course of three weeks, my wife and I stayed in North Carolina finalizing arrangements to get our son home to Maine for treatments. The miracles God performed through the special people I call "angels" to overcome obstacles to get Scott out of the state were tremendous. This chapter highlights not only the difficulties, but the amazing "angels" God used to help our desperate family, amid our fears and doubt.

Joe, Cheryl and Jamie Gaskin top my list of "angels." Before we even arrived in North Carolina, this family offered their home to us for as long as it was needed. Their home became a sanctuary for my wife, as well as my daughter Marnie and her husband Josue and son Judah to deal with Scott's medical needs under one roof. Marnie had met Jamie at Dallas Theological Seminary in Dallas, Texas while they both were getting their Master's degrees. With zero hesitation, their home became our sanctuary after a long day at Cape Fear Hospital or a full day getting Scott's affairs in order. For twelve days, we slept, ate and strategized in the home of 'strangers.' Nevertheless, the Gaskins treated like family.

Scott's primary doctor from Cape Fear Hospital, Dr. Okafor, is the next on my list of "angels." Before Scott was discharged from the hospital, he saw over a half a dozen doctors due to complications with his diagnosis. I won't go into all those complications, however, with complications come paperwork. Despite being nearly forty, Scott had no necessary power of attorney or living will papers drawn up; not helpful in this current age. Dr. Okafor stood out among her peers, as her willingness to assist our family through all the red tape. She understood our fears and frustrations, and began to assist us above and beyond the status quo. Whether records we needed for Scott's employer or ARMY Staff Sergeant, Dr. Okafor exceeded her job responsibilities to provide not only the best physical care, but emotional care as well.

Thirdly, Colonel James Martin's actions make him our next angelic encounter. When diagnosed, Scott was a reservist in the United States ARMY. In order for him to legally leave the state of North Carolina, he needed permission from his first sergeant. Marnie, Scott's sister and named power of attorney, had significant issues getting through the red tape of ARMY policies. That is until Marnie got in touch with Colonel Martin, Scott's great golfing buddy. Colonel Martin put her in touch with the right people in the right departments to complete the mission. The old adage is true: it's not what you know, but who you know. (I think of the angel that got Peter out of prison in Acts 12: 7)!

The next angel was Vivian Scott, one of the managers at Scott's bank, Navy Federal Credit. As events became clearer and the possibility of getting Scott home began to materialize, I knew I had to deal with Scott's finances. One Tuesday, I drove to Scott's bank to tell them our story, fully knowing I had no authority to do anything. Banking and privacy laws are worse than the medical laws. As I entered Ms. Scott's office, I had low expectations, but found an "angel." After sharing my story, she simply told me she couldn't help me, but she would! If asked she would deny everything, but she instantly got into her computer and settled everything with a few movements of her mouse. If you don't think these are miracles, or these people are not angels, I challenge you to try and do what we did for my son in a strange place with strange people who you don't know, or they don't know you!

Despite the amazing angels I've mentioned up until this point, the best and last one was Officer McKenzie McKoy. Earlier in the year Scott had gotten into trouble with the law. Due to the restrictions of his parole, he was not able to leave North Carolina state lines for one full year. It would have been illegal for my wife and me to take Scott to Maine for medical treatment. We pleaded with the Lord to intervene, and He did by sending us Officer McKoy. My daughter Marnie had been in touch with her from the beginning of our cancer journey, and had begun to work through the legal system maze of North Carolina. It took nearly two weeks with numerous ups and downs, including the judge demanding all the medical records (Dr. Okafor's help). Even then, the judge was only going to transfer Scott to a parole officer in Maine. One of the deepest and darkest days of our tribulation was when I heard that I might have to go to court and beg for mercy before this judge. Just like the widow of Jesus parable in Luke 18:1–6, we had someone pleading for us. From one of the deepest valleys of our time in North Carolina to one of the highest peaks, just one day before Coleen and Scott would board a private plane for Maine (wait until that story in the next chapter); Officer McKoy arrived on Scott's doorstep with good news. Not only had the judge listened to her, but he dropped all charges and restrictions against Scott! Officer McKoy is a young mother of four, but her support and advocacy for our son was like that of one of her own: a true "angel" unawares!

I have written a devotional book on all the angelic encounters recorded in the Bible, and I have studied angelology in depth. The greatest truth I have found about angels is this verse in Paul's letter to the Hebrews, "Are they not all ministering spirits sent forth to minister for those who shall be heirs of salvation?" (Hebrews 1:14) Space does not permit me to retell the stories attached to angels like Greg Odiorne, Daniel Ballock, the storage locker owner or the nurses on the sixth floor of Cape Fear Hospital. These ministering angels the Good Lord had in Fayetteville, North Carolina allowed our son to return home to Maine to receive treatment and spend his final days with family. Truly, angels unaware!

Chapter 9

A Flight for Scotty

PHONE CALLS RECEIVED AT five o'clock in the morning never contain good news. My family has received many cancer phone calls over the last twenty years. I will never forget any of them.

The first came from my father-in-law, Stacy Meister, in the spring of 1996. Stacy had been diagnosed with lung and liver cancer, interestingly the exact diagnosis his grandson would receive twenty years later. The second came from my wife Coleen, during the winter of 2005. Her annual mammogram revealed breast cancer. The third came during the summer of 2007 while on a mission's trip to India. My wife called to tell me her mother Opal had been diagnosed with colon cancer. The fourth call, perhaps the hardest of the four, came during the fall of 2016 from our only, son Scott.

Scott was barely thirty-eight years old at the time of the call. We doubted the diagnosis. We encouraged him to seek a second opinion through physicians at Veteran Affairs (VA) office. The VA doctor confirmed the diagnosis of stage four liver cancer and referred him to a civilian doctor. Without a biopsy, we still remained skeptical, praying for a different answer. On October 20, 2016, my wife and I drove from Maine, while my daughter Marnie and her family flew from California. We determined to find out together what road lay ahead of us. I made the longest hospital call in my forty-four years as a pastor—1050 miles in eighteen hour's time.

By the time we reached Fayetteville, NC, Marnie, her husband Josue and son Judah had arrived and had immediately taken Scott to the emergency room. Twenty-four hours later, his pain finally managed, we waited for a biopsy to understand exactly what form of cancer we were facing. The results revealed a high grade Neuroendocrine Carcinoma, a rapid moving cancer that typically originates in the lungs. Scott's pain was mainly in his liver, but we would soon learn the cancer has already spread to his adrenal glands, lymph nodes in his chest and the fifth vertebra on his spine. Another test would reveal a two inch tumor on his lung. Our boy was very sick, dying with a terminal disease that would likely take him within six months. We were shocked. Devastated! Disbelieving! Depressed!

Scott stayed in the hospital for twelve days getting his pain under control and receiving four rounds of chemotherapy. After only one month, Scott had lost forty-six pounds, and ten pounds after five days in the hospital. Needless to say, Scott was too sick and weak to endure an eighteen hour car ride home to Maine. We looked at a variety of flight options, including Angel Flights, but nothing was available.

Marnie and her family returned to California after ten days, and within two days of her departure we had Scott back to his apartment. Our next goal was to get him to Maine before needing his next round of chemotherapy (he was on a three day on, three weeks off regime). With all traditional means of travel seemingly coming up empty, Marnie remembered her former boss, owner of Aero-Tech Services, and a flight school and charter service company based out of Smoketown, Pennsylvania. After twelve years with no contact with my daughter, the owner, Matthew Kauffman, didn't hesitate to agree to fly to Fayetteville Regional Airport to pick-up my wife and son.

Four days later, we had transferred his care to an oncologist in Maine, received permission from the ARMY for Scott to take a medical leave of absence, and found someone to store his truck and motorcycle and belongings. The morning of November fourth, I drove Scott and Coleen to the Signature Air Support building on the grounds of the Fayetteville Regional Airport. Matt Kauffman arrived within the hour with his best plane, an executive eight passenger prop plane with leather seats. Two hours and forty-five minutes later, Coleen and Scott landed at the Trenton Airport, a mere ten miles from our home. Greg Bowden, a deacon from my church, met them at the airport, drove them home and helped my wife get Scott settled. I stood amazed at the miracle which occurred, not merely in the pieces of the puzzle that fell into place, but the generosity of the body of Christ. Matt Kauffman never charged us a cent for the flight! As I sought an answer for the dilemma we faced in Fayetteville, I remembered a favorite article I had placed in one of my prayer journals:

Beware in your prayers of limiting God, not only by unbelief, but by fancying that you know what He can do. Expect things above all that you ask or think. 2 Chronicles 25:9 reads, "The Lord is able to give thee much more than this." Ask largely, and thy God will be a kingly giver unto thee! Saints have never yet reached the limit to the possibilities of prayer. Whatever has been attained or achieved has touched but the fringe of the garment of the prayer-hearing God. We honor the riches both of His honor and of His power and love only by large demands. You cannot think of prayer so large that God, in answering it, will not wish that you had made it larger. Pray not for crutches, but for wings. (Plane's wings?)

Those words were written by Phillips Brooks, but uniquely applied to our desperate situation in Fayetteville, North Carolina. God gave the Blackstone family wings to fly home. I have also been touched with the words of this poem:

> Make thy petition deep,
> It is thy God who speaks with love overflowing,
> Thy God who claims the rapture of bestowing,
> Thy God who whispers, all thy weakness knowing, wouldst thus
> in full reap?
> Make thy petition deep. Make thy petition deep.
> Now to the fountain head thy vessel bringing,
> Claim all the fulness of its glad up springing;
> At Calvary was proclaimed its boundless measure;
> Who spared not them, withholds from thee no treasure;
> This word-His token, keep;
> Make thy petition deep!

We were filled to the uttermost, and yes even to running over. Paul said it best when he wrote, "Now unto Him that is able to do exceeding abundantly above all that we ask or think, according to the power that worketh in us" (Ephesians 3:20).

Chapter 10

Into the Valley of the Shadow of Death

THE FOLLOWING IS AN early morning entry my son Scott wrote while deployed to Afghanistan from 2010–2011. Little did he know what he and his buddies were riding into that day or how drastically their lives would change.

"August 25, 2011. Day 12 of my 13th mission. We have all the stuff we came for. We have dropped off all the loads that we had to deliver and today we are on our way back home to Leatherneck (his base). It is about 0423. I didn't sleep very well last night, maybe because I slept all day yesterday. But I am ready to leave and get back . . .then to do it over again! I have no idea what is in store for today; probably more IEDs (improvised explosive devices) or maybe a smooth ride home? Whatever happens: it was meant to be! Well I am pretty sure I will write later with exciting stuff to tell. I have to get the truck ready to leave anyway. We roll out at 0500. So this is Blackstone OUT!"

After nearly a year in Helmand Province, Afghanistan, Scott and his comrades knew of the dangers lurking amid the IED infested deserts they would travel to reach home base. They had travelled the road before and fully knew that their convoy was crawled through the 'valley of death.' As they inched through Taliban country, the unseen enemy waited to kill, for no reason other than a dead American was better than a living American. My wife and I watched the nightly news praying with each repeated list of those who gave the ultimate sacrifice that our son's name would not be among them. But, with his deployment coming to a close, we knew he was in serious danger on this last mission.

While Scott's unit planned their return to Camp Leatherneck, the Taliban sowed IED bombs along their route. ARMY engineers scouted the route before each convoy and found many of the landmines. However, they never could find them all. Despite the danger that lurked, Scott's company never hesitated to fulfill their mission. He knew the risk, but never considered cancelling the mission. The question remained, "Would our son be the next casualty?"

Scott did become a casualty on that trip, August 25, 2011, when an IED explosion detonated under the vehicle in front of Scott and his driving partner, Carrie Mabb. The explosion was so severe, the forward vehicle, along with Scott's two buddies, exploded and landed on top of his own vehicle. After sustaining possible life threatening concussions, he and Mabb were air-lifted back to their base. They would both earn the Purple Heart medal for their service that day.

Scott barely survived his trip through the Afghan valley of the shadow of death. He emerged with PTSD (posttraumatic stress disorder), a chronic brain injury and recurring nightmares of his friends burning to death before his eyes. But now Scott has entered a second valley of death, but this time going through it would look much different. It is not in some trackless desert setting in Helmand, Afghanistan, but in a recliner in the living room of the parsonage of the Emmanuel Baptist Church in Ellsworth, Maine.

As I write these words, my beloved son lies gravely ill. It is day 160 of this vigil. Just as my wife and I awaited news from Afghanistan that he had made it through another mission, we wait and pray. Scott will get through this valley of death as well, but what he reaches on the other side will be far greater. There will be no more PTSD. No more head trauma. No more nightmares. No more chemotherapy treatments. No more pain. The apostle John was clear in his revelation about this when he writes, "He will wipe away every tear from their eyes. There will be no more death or mourning or crying or pain." (Revelation 7:17, 21:4)

Chapter 11

Out of the Valley of the Shadow of Death

As SCOTT WALKS FURTHER into the valley of the shadow of death, he nears the sixth anniversary of his closest call to death on a HETS mission in Helmand Province Afghanistan. The warrior that survived that Taliban IED is still haunted by the things he saw and the terrible events he experienced. While he might not have any visible bullet wounds or shrapnel scars, there are plenty of invisible reminders of his days in Helmand. The price he paid to fight one of America's wars, the longest in US history, will not be forgotten.

These memories of my soldier son have prompted smiles and tears, but also a warm swagger that has allowed me to hold my head high. I desire others to know of his story, a story that happened to thousands of American soldiers like him. I want to tell the story of a simple soldier who endured horrifying battlefield experiences and returned home, as so many did, with posttraumatic stress and survivor's guilt; a soldier who returned to civilian life to live a life worthy of any survivor. I want the reader to understand the legacy of a willing warrior who has found that while the IEDs have stop exploding, the noise and the death and screams are still clearly heard. Flashbacks and nightmares lessen as the sweet remembrances of camaraderie with the men and women who shared the hell of Helmand with him are recalled.

What was once labeled "shell shock" and "battle fatigue" after the First World War has been accurately labeled "PTSD (post-traumatic stress disorder)." Society is only beginning to scratch the surface in understanding the lasting effects of war on a person's psyche. After finding the courage to fight through Taliban explosions, Scott has also found the courage to fight through the headaches and the depression and the trauma and the tragedy of war. I am so proud of my son and his willingness to find help after his return. The physical effect of three battlefield concussions are getting better, but the memory loss and the times of confusion remains. Scott's emotional wounds are healing as well, but the scars will remain. They are now part of his life and have helped to create the man Scott has become.

Scott never went to war for the medals, but simply to honor his family and his nation. Scott came out of these wars with numerous medals and awards including:

- For exceptional meritorious service while serving as a gun truck crewman during Iraqi Freedom 07–09. SPC Blackstone's dedication to duty and professionalism made him an invaluable asset to his unit. His actions reflected great credit upon himself, the 4th Sustainment Brigade, and the United States Army, from July 26, 2007 to October 23, 2008.

- For exceptional meritorious service while tasked to the 7th Transportation Battalion (Airborne) Support Operations as an Outload Support Team Provider from October 22, 2009 thru October 29, 2009. His dedication to duty enabled the 7th Transportation Battalion (Airborne) support operations to complete all assigned tasks and operations successfully. His diligence and outstanding performance reflected great credit upon himself, the unit, the 7th Transportation Battalion (Airborne), the 82nd Sustainment Brigade and the United States Army.

- For exceptional meritorious achievement as an instructor and participant in second platoon, 126th Transportation Company's six week training cycle. Specialist Blackstone's tactical expertise and warrior ethos greatly enhanced the platoon's ability to conduct combat operations. His outstanding performance reflects great credit upon himself, the 330th Transportation Battalion, and the United States Army, from August 24, 2009 to October 2, 2009.

- For exceptionally meritorious service as a convoy security element vehicle commander and heavy equipment transport operator in support of Operation Enduring Freedom 11–12. His outstanding performance, dedication to duty and selfless service greatly contributed to the overall Unit's mission success. His distinctive accomplishments reflect great credit upon himself, 7th Sustainment Brigade and the United States Army, from October 23, 2010 to October 22, 2011.

- For meritorious service while assigned as a heavy Vehicle driver in support of Operation Enduring Freedom. Specialist Blackstone's dedication to duty, professionalism, and motivation are keeping with the finest traditions of military service and reflect great credit upon himself, the 751st Combat Sustainment Battalion, the 371st Sustainment Brigade, and the United States Army, from July 6, 2013 to April 1, 2014.

- For meritorious achievement in the support of the rescue of a civilian worker on October 7, 2011. Specialist Blackstone distinguished himself by displaying the utmost professionalism and dedication to duty in his contributing to the successful rescue. His accomplishments are in keeping with the finest traditions of the military and reflect great credit upon himself, the 546th Transportation Company, the 375th Combat Sustainment Battalion, and the United States Army.

I am honored to call this soldier, who sacrificed more than most, my son.

Chapter 12

Back into the Valley of the Shadow of Death

SCOTT PENNED THE FOLLOWING words, as the conclusion to his *HETS in Helmand* book. His words are chilling considering his current battle:

"On October 18, 2011, I walked across the tarmac at Camp Leatherneck to catch my first flight to take me home to Maine. At the top of the ramp, I paused for a few seconds to breathe in the dusty desert air of Afghanistan that had been my home for nearly a year. I scanned the hills to the east and recalled the countless missions to those hills that crawled with the enemy, an enemy still being held back by the brave and courageous soldiers of the United States. A silent prayer of thanksgiving escaped my lips that I had made it out alive, yet continually wondered why some had lost their lives; my four battle buddies had died in those hills. I would never forget them.

My uneasy confrontation with God continues, as I again pondered the friends I have lost in those empty desert fields of IEDs. I saw no death during my deployment to Iraq. Afghanistan was a different story. I meditated on the randomness of death and God's choices. Why spare my life, but not theirs? Why were their lives taken, but not mine? These questions haunt me daily.

I willingly volunteered to join the ARMY during wartime. The war was controversial, as most tend to be. I never debated the right or wrong of it. I left the debate to others. My motives were pure. I went to the sandbox as a soldier with a mission to help those on the frontlines. I soon realized my missions would put me on the frontlines, as well.

One of the reasons I chose to keep a journal during these days was to highlight and underline what the average soldier saw, experienced and felt during deployment. Questions like, "why me?" and "why not me?" plague us. I daily deal with the guilt of being a survivor, despite my own PTSD moments. Nightmares leave me shaken every time. Anger issues lead me to trouble I otherwise would not find. But, I have never used my war time experiences as an excuse for my actions. I am slowly learning that so much of PTSD comes back to the realization that I lived and my friends died. While therapy helps, I must also come to terms that mentally and physically, I may never escape the memories of watching my buddies burning to death in their blown up HETS.

Although I left Afghanistan with all my body parts, I also know I left a piece of my heart, soul and mind. A piece of my heart remains in the land due to my spiritual connection to the men I saw killed. A piece of my soul remains because of my desperation to depend on my God during my days there. A piece of my mind remains because no matter how hard I try, I can never get the hellish land out of my thoughts. Afghanistan, try as I might, will remain a part of who I am forever. I end this journal understanding now more than ever that "the sandbox" shaped the man I am today, for better and for worse. I cannot escape it. May these observations of a simple soldier, a combat driver, bring insight to the soldiers in your life and all they might face."

I finished compiling Scott's *HETS in Helmand* book the same month he received his cancer diagnosis. Little did I know that within sixty months of this book's conclusion, he would fight a greater battle than Afghanistan. My wife and I feared that Scott would never return to us from the battlefield. Now, his life is not cut short by a Taliban IED, but rather High Grade Neuroendocrine Carcinoma, a disease that would overtake his body within six months. Coleen and I have often said death on the battlefield might have been easier for us. A sniper's shot would be quick, rather than the slow, agonizing suffering of cancer. Death regardless of the method is painful, and so we wait for the Lord to answer our questions as to his methods later.

We face the valley of the shadow of death once more. After thirteen combat missions in Afghanistan and twenty-five combat missions in Iraq, we understand what waiting for the call of safety or suffering requires. We knew that each mission could have been his last. We never dreamed we would be on his last mission with him. The battlefield has become our living room and the Taliban tumors are sniping away at our son's vital organs. I am not sad about where my lad is heading. I actually envy him and the glory that awaits! However, I do not envy the sadness that awaits my wife and daughter in these final days.

Distance has a way of shielding one from the trauma, but there is no shielding us during this valley journey. Scott wants to die with us present; a far more traumatic event than a call or knock on the door from uniformed soldiers. Our only source of comfort and consolation is the promise given by David when he wrote of the valley of the shadow of death in these informative words, "Yea, though I walk through the valley of the shadow of death, I will fear no evil: for thou art with me, they rod and thy staff they comfort me" (Psalm 23:4). I was reading an explanation on Psalm 23:4 and the author explained this verse this way,

> Yea: (My Journey) *though I walk through the valley of the shadow*
> *of death*: (My Courage)
> *I will fear no evil:* (My Companion) *for Thou art with me*: (My
> Comfort) *Thy rod and thy staff*: Praise the Lord!

Amid our journey, we find courage in the companionship and comfort of the Lord alone. Praise the Lord He walks beside us through the Valley of the Shadow of Death.

Chapter 13

A Fake Forest

I FIND MYSELF WRITING again amid Scott's struggle and questioning what is reality and what is false. Learning my son has cancer at age thirty-eight seemed so unreal, yet it is true. Even now, facing week twenty-three of this disease, it seems to be a dream. As I sit in my office, all seems normal. One short walk across the street reveals my only son wasting away before my eyes. When I turned forty, I wrote a series of remembrances. This morning I opened that book again and found an amazing parallel I would like to share with you now.

"After school last Friday, I took Scott and Marnie to the big city of Bangor for some shopping. As I waited in the Maine Mall for them, my eyes fell upon man's attempting to bring a forest inside. Synthetic shade shrubs planted in a spacious mecca of merchandising. There are some authentic trees thrown amid the fake, but I bemoan the businessman trying to peddle the phony.

The inside forest has been around for years, but what a pitiful substitute they are. I sat for a while the other day under one of these so called 'havens of hardwood,' only to feel sorry for those who have never ever been to a real forest or sat under a real shade tree. Those who create these malls have limited vision for what really makes up a forest; it is the difference between man-made and God-made.

I grew up in the fields and forests of rural northern Maine. My hallowed homestead contained more woodland than farmland. My childhood echoes the stories of days in the forest partridge hunting, strolling under the spruce, dreaming under the fir trees, riding bikes through miles of forest to school and strolling under the maples with my favorite girl. No comparison exists between man's attempts to replicate the real forest.

We live in "the century of the counterfeit"; synthetic spruce should not take us by surprise. They seem real, genuine, and authentic. At times, they look better than the real ones. I come to the same conclusion as my favorite author Vance Havner, 'No city product can really capture the spirit of the hills!' Only those who are colonists of the country can understand the speech of the spruce. The more I walk in their artificial forest, the more I feel like an exile, an alien from the real world where I once lived. My feet might have to occasionally tread through manmade green, but my forty year old heart will never accept these imaginary imitations."

One of the dangers I believe we face as we fight cancer is the danger of believing this can't be real. My son has terminal cancer, and I believe his days are numbered unless the Great Physician chooses to intervene. But I also believe that in times like this we forget this admonition from the pen of Paul, "For which cause we faint not; but though our outward man perish, yet the inward man is renewed day by day. For our light affliction, which is but for a moment, worketh for us a far more exceeding and eternal weight of glory. While we look not at the things which are seen, but at the things which are not seen: for the things which are seen are temporal; but the things which are not seen are eternal" (II Corinthians 4:16–18).

I have come to believe that if an individual cannot turn to God in the hour of their deepest need, saddest sorrow, and greatest sadness, their faith is very small. If I cannot come boldly before his throne of grace in my time of loss, then what is truly real is in fact false, and what is false has deceived me at my greatest hour (Hebrews 4:16). One of the evil one's greatest desires is to switch the believer's focus from the eternal to the temporal, from God's wisdom to man's perspective. When we do this, we fail to see God's hand at work amid our trial. Our eyes see only the withering and wasting away of flesh and bones, and not God's way of departure for my son. The apostle Paul wrote, ". . .for the fashion of this world passeth away" (I Corinthians 7:31). This is not the time to change our walk in Christ because our nerves are failing or our flesh is weakening.

King David wrote, "Why art thou cast down, O my soul? And why art thou disquieted in me? Hope thou in God: for I shall yet praise Him for the help of His countenance" (Psalm 42:5,11). We must believe that our God and his Son, Jesus Christ are not fair-weather friends. I testify that He is accessible and available. The wise man Solomon said regarding life and living, "To everything there is a season and a time to every purpose under heaven: a time to be born and *a time to die*. . ." (Ecclesiastes 3:1–2). Life is a series of 'times.' During each one, we must be careful to discern between the real and fake life. There are those among us who are walking around dead, yet with no terminal diagnosis. The popular misconception is that to be alive is to be breathing. Yet, the apostle Paul speaks of those who ". . .were dead in trespasses and sins" (Ephesians 2:1). The context of Paul's verses in the book of Ephesians is to those walking around living and active life, enjoying the world around them, but in reality are dead spiritually. More people than we care to recognize believe they have unlimited time to eat, drink and be merry. This is the fake news! The Bible conveys ". . .it is appointed unto men once to die. . ." (Hebrews 9:27). The medical profession would keep us alive and the Devil convinces so many they will live forever; they will, but in a place only prepared for the Devil and his angels (Matthew 25:41). Watch out for the fake!

Chapter 14

God Made a Farmer

I HAD THE HONOR of preaching at my father's funeral. I shared with the congregation that I had come that day wearing three hats: a shepherd's hat, a surrogate's hat and a son's hat. I wore the hat of a shepherd seeking to comfort and encourage the flock before me as they journeyed on in their grief. I wore the hat of a surrogate, as I preached portions of an old sermon my father had written years prior (see chapter two). I wore the hat of a son, for I would share the depths of what my Dad had meant to me. My memorial followed the Apostle Paul's outline in 2 Timothy 2:1–15, in which my father was known as a *son* (1–2), *soldier* (3–4), *sprinter* (5), *sower* (6) and *student* (15). My father, Wendell Blackstone, spent his life sowing the fields of Perham, Maine. As a potato farmer, you could always find him on his John Deere tending to the land. I was given the following article, which so accurately summarizes my Dad:

"And on the eighth day, God looked down on His divine creation and said, 'I need a caretaker!' (Genesis 2:8) So God made a farmer. God said: 'I need somebody willing to get up before dawn, milk the cows, work all day in the fields, milk the cows again, eat supper and then go to town and stay past midnight at the meeting of the town selectmen of Perham. So God made a farmer. He said, 'I need somebody with arms powerful enough to wrestle a Holstein into submission and yet gentle enough to hold a great-grandchild named Judah Alan.' So God made a farmer. And God said, 'I need somebody to call the hogs, control the dogs, tame the cantankerous machinery of the farm, come home hungry, but leave before he has had his lunch because a neighbor was in need!' So God made a farmer. God said, 'I need somebody willing to sit up all night with a newborn calf and watch it die in the morning; then dry his tears, and say: 'maybe next year?' I need somebody who can shape an ax handle from an ash branch, sharpen the blade, and then wield it against a mighty oak to provide firewood for his family.' So God made a farmer. God said, 'I need somebody who can make do with whatever was at hand; to make do and do with little time and far little money; who, planting time and harvest time, will finish his 40-hour week by Tuesday noon. Then, paining from 'tractor back' will put in another 72 hours before the week is through.' So God made a farmer. God said, 'He needed somebody willing to ride the ruts at double-speed to get the hay in ahead of the rain clouds, to get the Katahdins (potatoes) in before the first frost, and to get the oats in before a damaging wind, and when his work was done go and help a fellow-farmer get his crops in.' So God made a farmer. God said, 'I need somebody strong enough to clear trees and heave bales and yet tender enough to raise five children equally, and who would stop mowing, plowing, or spraying for an hour to rest at noon.' So God made a farmer. It had to be somebody who would plow deep and straight and not cut corners; somebody to seed, weed, feed, breed; somebody to rake and disc and plow and plant and tend the herd and strain the milk and replenish the self-feeder in the chicken coup, and finish a hard week's work with a three mile drive to the Perham Baptist Church on Sunday and Wednesday. So God made a farmer. Somebody who would bind a family together with the soft, strong bonds of God's love and the Truth of the Word of God. Who could laugh and then sighed, and then reply with smiling eyes when his middle son would say he wanted to spend his life doing what his dad had done! So God made a farmer. God made Wendell E. Blackstone."

If asked to describe my father in one word, it would be the word "farmer." In the rural community of Northern Maine, there were many who farmed, but few farmers existed among them. Well into his eighties, my Dad was still at the plow. I think one of his most loved responsibilities on the farm was plowing. Every autumn, after the completion of potato harvest, my Dad plowed the gleaned fields in preparation for the next season. I remember the first fall dad took me to the top of the hill above my grandparent's home and instructed me in the fine art of plowing. "The plow must be pulled, son, not pushed." Vance Havner would say: *"A lot of energy can be spent trying to push what can only be pulled!"* "Now son," my father said, "Remember, it is our responsibility to guide and the tractor's responsibility to pull." The art of keeping the plow straight in the furrow found success only by determining his course by the tall spruce tree at the end of the field. "Keep your eye on the goal, Barry, " Dad would say. If I was to plow a straight furrow I could not be distracted by the plow or another tractor. Whether guiding work horses in the early days or maneuvering his John Deere, his patience and precision never failed. There was never a farmer who could plant a straighter row or plow a more precise furrow than Wendell E. Blackstone. My father's life mirrored the precision of his plowed fields, straight and true to his course. He gave everything to the farm, whether thirty below zero mid-winter or blazing sun mid-summer. The farm came first. Why? Because my Dad embodied a farmer. The apostle Paul likens us to a farm when he writes, "You are God's field" (1 Corinthians 3:9). God is the tender, precise farmer who lovingly tends to his children and their needs. Whether fields of joy or sorrow, our heavenly Father cares for us. I remain eternally grateful to have been given an earthly father who so mirrors my Heavenly Father.

Chapter 15

Valley Comrades

If forty is the number for testing, then a 'valley' is the symbol for testing (Psalm 23:4). When I turned 40 years of age, I wrote some articles on my thoughts and reflections of turning forty. As we travel with Scott through his fortieth year and the cancer that is testing him, I find it interesting that what I wrote twenty-six years ago is so helpful now.

"I began my day off this morning with the hope the day would yield a vision for my brother Jay, who took over the Blackstone homestead from our father. I wanted to dream a dream for him, or at least find a revelation to the difficulty he faces. The morning has come and gone. The afternoon is far spent with no inspiration or answers. I remember a writer who once spent a night in the Garden of Gethsemane, seeking rare inspiration in such a momentous location. After his night all he could write of the experience was 'a dull and most ordinary night.' More often than not, God uses the drab and difficult places to inspire us. Paul penned his epistles not from the deck of a cruise ship on a Mediterranean journey, but the depths of a dark, damp Roman jail. Perhaps therein lays the wisdom for my brother Jay, as he chooses to remain farming the homestead or sell the land?

With this day is almost gone, I am struck that I have been looking for inspiration in the wrong place. Rather than trying to change the situation my beloved homestead is in, I should be trying to find inspiration in its history. The answer comes not in change, but in adjustment to change. Vance Havner once said, *"We cannot control the wind, but we can adjust to it, and set up our windmills and wait. What matters most is faithfulness, in season and out, feel like it or not, vision or no vision."* Moses found God where he was, not where he went. Too often I have tried to find God and inspiration by searching on my own for the blessing, only to discover upon my return the blessing was in the place I left.

The boys and girls raised on the Blackstone farm have gone forth for six generations. A seventh generation now grows. Let us never forget that the greatest harvest the homestead ever has produced was its kids not its crops. Whether the homestead remains a dairy and potato farm is not the question. As long as there is faithfulness to God and His Word, each generation will harvest another generation and such continue the legacy of faithfulness and fruitfulness of the Blackstone Homestead."

Years have passed since I penned these words, yet the desire for inspiration remains. I now seek revelation for my son and the plight he finds himself in. My brother Jay left the farm to attend college and became a Junior High history teacher. The farm has been sold off piece by piece to Amish families setting in Northern Maine from Pennsylvania. All I pondered and worried over almost twenty-five years ago, has worked out well. I believe the same will be true for my son. When you are in the midst of the valley, the only thing you are confident in is the place where you entered. The exit is still to be determined.

Despite the unknowns ahead, I have learned that Scott and my family don't walk the valley alone. I call them 'valley comrades' or 'valley pilgrims'; those who have trod on before us and with us through tragedy, embracing our bereavement and strolling in our suffering. Just yesterday, a dear pastor friend of mine came by for a visit. We've spent years serving the Lord together just across town from each other. While he made it clear he couldn't fully understand what my wife and I are enduring, he offered prayer and support and the knowledge he walked with us. He knows what I have learned: what a person cannot understand through imagination or observation, does not forbid him from walking together with another.

Scott seems to hang onto life by a thread each day. With each passing day, I discovered the "valley of the shadow of death" is not lonely, but actually very crowded. I never dreamed there would be so many in this dark valley. And for each that walks with us, there is another multitude that has passed before us. We have joined the ancient fraternity of the brokenhearted, veterans of the war against cancer and partners in the struggle to understand the why's of God.

The Bible speaks of the multitude that has come out of tribulation, testing, and trial. One day, my wife and I will join that society. We will not speculate, philosophize, or use clichés when we meet others affected by cancer. We will have first-hand knowledge learned only in the valley.

My Lord and Savior is a member of this valley club. Isaiah 53:3 writes, ". . .a man or sorrows, and acquainted with grief. . .." Did anyone walk through a darker valley than He? No. Did He walk alone? No. His Father walked with Him, as I walk with my son. Jesus' valley ended in death (Philippians 2:8), and it appears so will my son's valley.

The price of membership into this 'valley' club is heartache and tears, despair and depression, and sleepless nights and mental anguish. There is, however, also companionship and comradeship beyond explanation. Jesus and a host of others have joined us in our journey we know this valley is not endless, but for as long as we endure it, we shall never walk alone.

Chapter 16

Hunger and a Thirst

DURING SCOTT'S SIX-MONTH BATTLE with lung cancer, hunger has been an issue. In fact, I would say Scott has only said he was truly hungry a few times. His lack of hunger has resulted in him becoming a mere shadow of his former self. He is flesh and bone. An additional side effect of his cancer has been an insatiable thirst. Despite the gallons of water he drinks, his body flushes his system with no benefit, depriving him of even the benefit of water. God created our bodies with a hunger impulse in order to give our bodies the fuel needed to be healthy. Regular nourishment and hydration are crucial to survival. Whatever reserves Scott had before he started this cancerous road are gone. After one hundred and sixty days with no appetite, he has withered away. This is one of the worst sights I have seen in my pastoral life, and I have seen some terrible things.

The Bible uses the image of "hunger" and "thirst" in some very interesting spiritual and physical applications. In Jesus' third beatitude from the Sermon on the Mount, he instructs us saying, "Blessed are they which do hunger and thirst after righteousness: for they shall be filled" (Matthew 5:6). A spiritual hunger and thirst are essential to daily life. However, the cancer known as sin has distorted our cravings. Paul writes of this in Romans when he says, "Let not sin therefore reign in your mortal body, that ye should obey it in the lusts thereof. Neither yield ye your members as instruments of unrighteousness unto sin: but yield yourselves unto God, as those that are alive from the dead, and your members as instruments of righteousness unto God" (6:12–13). Sin starves and dehydrates us from the spiritual

45

nourishment we find in the righteousness of God. Jesus humbled himself and came to earth in order to die for the unrighteousness that is starving us. Paul writes, "For He has made Him to be sin for us, who knew no sin; that we might be made the righteousness of God in Him" (II Corinthians 5:21). The prophet Isaiah uses this same imagery when he writes of the children of Israel, "They shall not hunger or thirst; neither shall the heat nor sun smite them: for He that hath mercy on them will lead them, even by the springs of water will he guide them" (Isaiah 49:10); whether physically or spiritually, the analogy of hunger and thirst is applicable in our travels with Scott through this valley of cancer (Matthew 25:42, 44, John 6:35, II Corinthians 11:27).

I will probably never be a modern success story or poster child for the way life should be lived. I am not a typical go-getter. I have no ambition to the best. I have never been the hurrying type looking for a bigger challenge. From my days as a boy in Perham, Maine until now, I have only had one "hunger" and "thirst." I lived in an age when there was time to stop beside the road to pick a dandelion, to listen to the tree sparrows sing, and to watch the splendid silence of a sunset. Today, I live in a city where the frantic pace is so intense I don't always get the time to enjoy the beauty surrounding me. My eyes are often fixed on the imaginary goal set before me by others who think life is all about doing. Sometimes I ask myself, "Why such a rush? Where are we going?" There is nothing at the end of this social race but high blood pressure, an ulcer, a heart attack, or insomnia, or all of the above. Life is already so fast. Why should we be in a hurry to go nowhere and to get anywhere?

I am not a city-boy built for speed, but a country boy built for steady. I am not aggressive. I do not take the initiative. I am a plodder. I am old fashioned and come from an era when sunrises and songbirds spoke louder than stocks and bonds. I hunger and thirst again for a good dose of spruce-spiced air, the lure of a loon on the lake, the serenity of a creek-side cabin, the tonic of taters (potatoes), the thrill of the first snow and the melody of a meadow choir of swallows.

When I was a lad, a railroad track ran across the bottom of the hill near my home. The train tracks have long since been torn up and with it the simple sign that stood as a warning to cars to "STOP! LOOK! LISTEN!" Ever once and awhile, I take seriously the message of that simple sign, lest I become a physical or mental wreck on the roadbed of life. I stop, as I did today, to reevaluate the speed I am going. I rearrange my priorities and reflect back to a time when the workload was great, but the perspective was simple. I look, as I did today, at the whole picture and realize that to watch the pageantry of changing of seasons is as important as anything else I do.

I listen, as I did today, to the wind blowing through the barren trees and to the sound of the migrating birds preparing for winter. This is as important to my sanity as a quiet day alone. While I have never been a good listener, the old sign reminds me I must heed its warning lest I be run over by a passing problem.

Have you learned how to stop amid the scrambling? Have you learned to look through the lunacy? Have you learned to listen to the lessons of life the Good Lord is trying to teach you; hunger and thirst, not for the applause of men, but the approval of God (Colossians 3:22–24; Hebrews 11:6). May my hunger and thirst during this trial with Scott be found pleasing to the Lord?

Chapter 17

Expendable: A Sacrificial Son

CAN YOU IMAGINE BEING called "laughter?" This was the meaning of Abraham and Sarah's son Isaac's name. His name served as a reminder to his aging parents of their laughter when they heard the angel's prediction of his birth despite their old age. Faith eventually took hold in Isaac's parents and the child of promise was born (Hebrews 11:11; Romans 4:19–20). Each time they called his name, Abraham and Sarah were reminded of their day of doubt. Years later, Abraham would be asked to make the greatest sacrifice ever asked of a human—sacrifice his only son.

Do you have anything or anyone in your life that reminds you of God's faithfulness and your faithfulness to him? Abraham learned on the mountain of Moriah that what God gives, He can also take back. God instructed Abraham, "And He said, Take now thy son, thine only son Isaac, whom you love, and get thee into the land of Moriah; and offer him there for a burnt offering upon one of the mountains which I will tell thee of" (Genesis 22:2).

It is not hard to imagine that Isaac quickly became the pride and joy of his father and mother after his miraculous conception and birth. (Isaac would have been thirty-seven at the time of Sarah's death in Genesis 23:1 and seventy-five at the time of Abraham's death in Genesis 27:7). Despite beginning their family late in life, both Abraham and Sarah were able to enjoy Isaac for many years, and that is what makes the sacrifice of Isaac such a trial of faith (Hebrews 11:17–19). Isaac was not only their "only begotten son," but also a son "in whom they were well pleased!" Sound familiar? I believe, in this story, we have a picture of the great trial of God the Father. When God sent his son Jesus to earth, the trial was much greater than what Abraham faced on Mount Moriah or even what my wife and I face today. God the Father sacrificed His Son for the redemption of mankind on Calvary.

Often times, we read the trial of Abraham in Hebrews 11:17 as affecting only Abraham himself. However, Sarah and Isaac remained greatly affected in their own unique ways as well. I believe Sarah was fully aware of what Abraham set out to do on Mount Moriah. Mothers have a keen sense of things, especially with their only son. My wife Coleen is struggling with Scott's cancer differently than I am. The slow death of her firstborn is nothing short of excruciating for her. But, the one we often overlook in this story is Isaac himself, being laid on an altar of sacrifice. Could we possibly ever know what went through his mind on that altar? What we must see in this story is the "Jehovah-Jireh—the Lord will provide" (Gen 22:14) and the Lord God's promise to provide a substitute for Isaac, so Abraham would not need to kill his own son.

Theologian F.B. Meyer writes on the trials of faith and I believe summarizes what my family and I need to hear:

"It was with an unfaltering tone that the patriarch [Abraham] told the young men that they two would presently return (Genesis 22: 5). Even though he should actually take Isaac's life, he was sure that he would receive him again from the altar in health. (Hebrews 11:19) It was only at the very last moment that God indicated (Genesis 22:10) the ram as the sufficient substitute. So God's deliverances always come; they are provided in the mount of trial and sacrifice. When the foe seems secure of victory! So it was with Israel, Pharaoh, with his hosts, counted on an easy victory, the precipices around, the sea in front. To the eye of sense it seemed impossible to escape; all hope died! It was just then that the Almighty created a path through the mighty deep: (Exodus 14) then there was what happened to the disciples 'in the fourth hour of the night!' Strength was well-nigh exhausted in the long battling with the waves. For hours the disciples with difficulty had kept themselves afloat. It seemed as if they must give in through physical collapse (a place my wife and I find ourselves in after six months). It was then that the form of Jesus drew nigh unto the ship. (Matthew 14) Or what about that night before execution! Thus Peter lies sleeping whilst the Church is gathered in prayer. Tomorrow he will be a corpse. But the angel (our hope the angel will soon come for son-Luke 16:22) comes then to open the prison doors. (Acts 12) So you many have come to an end of your own strength, and wisdom, and energy. The altar, the wood, and fire are ready, the knife is raised, your Isaac on the point to die; but even now God will provide. Trust Him to indicate the way of escape (I Corinthians 10:13)." Amen and Amen!

How often Coleen and I have found that strength and energy and wisdom to handle this trial of cancer with our son? The greatest lesson I have learned from Abraham, Sarah and Isaac, is the amazing parallels to what my God and His Son endured for me. Isaac was a beloved son, as was Jesus (as is Scott; Genesis 22:2-John 3:16). Isaac was a questioning son, as was Jesus (as is Scott; Genesis 22:7-Matthew 26:39). Isaac was a yielding son, as was Jesus (as is Scott; Genesis 22:9-Matthew 26:42). Abraham and Isaac exhibited tremendous faith on Mount Moriah. God's great love for his children was exhibited when He offered His own Son as a substitute. God is no "Indian giver." He does, however, see his gifts to us as expendable, as He molds his children into His image. Through my study of "expendable" things, I have come to believe that God will not always ask us to sacrifice, but He does ask us to be willing to sacrifice. I recognize that God is using my son's sickness for some divine molding and shaping of my life and the lives of those around Scott. It is my prayer that we will come forth as gold in our trial of sacrifice (I Peter 1:7)!

Chapter 18

Divine Chastisement or Devilish Cancer?

At the time of my son's cancer diagnosis, I was teaching on the book of Job to a group of adults from my church, Emmanuel Baptist in Ellsworth, Maine. While I had studied the book ten years prior, I felt the content to be a difficult topic and delayed teaching until I had a better understanding of its makeup and meaning. Even after compiling handout sheets outlining the forty-two chapters, I still hesitated on teaching the deep doctrine of why God allows the righteous to suffer? But, after so much preparation, I picked up the book and my research notes and took the plunge. While I still believe it to be the most difficult book to teach in the Old Testament, I clearly see God's hand bringing me to a place of personal tragedy so I might understand and explain the book in a more realistic and practical way.

After studying the Bible for nearly half a century, I believe the Bible speaks of two sides of suffering: chastening or fashioning. The Bible is very clear that "For whom the Lord loves He chastens, and scourges every son whom He receives" (Hebrews 12:6). But the Bible is equally clear that: "Wherein ye greatly rejoice, though now for a season, if need be, ye are in heaviness through manifold temptations: that the trial of your faith, being much more precious than of gold. . ." (I Peter 1:6–7). When any Christian endures a trial like my family is experiencing, we pause to wonder if it is a fashioning from God or a diabolical attack from the wicked one. A careful reading of Job 1–2 reveals, it is neither one nor the other, but both! Further research into the stories of the Bible unravel, the mystery that has haunted Christians for centuries: why do bad things happen to good people?

Here are a few Biblical examples of suffering attributed to Satan. Job's afflictions, both personally (the loss of his family and fortune, Job 1) and physically (the loss of his health and heritage, Job 2), were administered directly from the hands of Satan after receiving direct permission from the Almighty Himself (1:12, 2:4–6). Paul believed his thorn in the flesh to a messenger of Satan (2 Corinthians 12:7). Jesus told an audience at the synagogue that a woman in their midst, "whom Satan has bound for eighteen years," should be loosed of her binds on the Sabbath (Luke 13:16).

While Satan is limited by the restrictions of God, Job's story teaches us that the Lord gives leeway to afflict the righteous (Job 1:1). While I face the loss of my only son, Job lost all ten of his children to a wind storm (Job 1:9). My wife and I lost a child between Scott and Marnie. The loss of that child devastated us, as if we had met the little one face to face. My lot is a hard one, but there are many who have endured greater testing. After nearly six months to ponder "why," I am convinced that my son's cancer is God's permissive will. Scott could have never been afflicted with Neuroendocrine Carcinoma without the Almighty's permission. I believe God is in control of all decisions, even if He allows Satan's hands to be used in the execution of said illness.

One question remains, however. Is this a chastening of my son or me or both (Hebrews 12:5–11)? I, like Job, defend my uprightness of heart and character. Only the Lord will reveal a transgression. Paul does say He comes to "sons" and not "bastards," and this is the best news of the tragedy. God does not hate us. God loves us! We will advance through this grievous time, and the afterward of this valley (Hebrews 12:11). Paul writes, "And we know that all things (including cancer) work together for good to them that love God, to those who are called according to His purpose." (Romans 8:28)." Read through to the end of the book of Job and you too will see the purpose of God, and the good that happened because of this trial (Job 42). In the devil's attempt to disrupt our faith, detour our hope, and deceive our trust, forgets that *God only takes on a challenge He knows He can win!*

I began my teaching of the book of Job by telling my students Job's story was not of a man trusting his God, but God trusting His man. The good Lord knows how cruel the Devil can be and what Satan would do to His servant Job. Yet, God allowed it, knowing Job would endure. Paul speaks of this when he says, ""There hath no temptation taken you but such as is common to man: but God is faithful, who will not suffer you to be tempted above that ye are able: but will with the temptation also make a way to escape, that ye may be able to bear it" (I Corinthians 10:13). God knew how far Job could be pushed. God knows how far He can push the Blackstones. Whether the Devil attacks our bodies, minds, health, wealth, or loved ones to discourage or divert us from our calling, God knows our breaking point. He will not allow Satan to go beyond that point.

What has often fascinated me of the Story of Job is the opening scene when God holds court with His angels and Satan is there. Satan understand the only way around Job's hedge of protection was permission from his Creator (Job 1:10). We are told in the book of Revelation that Satan accuses the saints daily (Revelation 12:10). Our Biblical knowledge tells us that we wrestle not with humanity, but the demonic forces of the unseen world (Ephesians 6:12) . Why then are we surprised by a satanic assault, or a devilish attack? Is our family under divine chastisement or a devilish siege? I believe we are under siege from the evil one. Should you ever be afflicted or someone you love be under affliction, accept God's will in the midst of it all. Embrace His sovereignty as seen in Job's story (Job 1:12). Whether Scott's name was discussed in heaven or not, I do not know. However, like Job, I know Scott's test will be for but a season (1 Peter 1:6). Job's story ends in a true happily ever after, and it is my belief that when all is said and done, Scott's story will end the same as well.

Chapter 19

Seeking Understanding

WHENEVER THE GOOD LORD decides to throw a curveball into your path, the normal response is to seek a better understanding as to the *what* and the why of it all. Since my childhood, I have been taught the principle of Psalms 119:104, "Through Thy precepts I get understanding. . .." I go, then, to the Word of God and childhood teachings to better understand why my son Scott contracted cancer at age thirty-eight.

Do you ever feel at times that life is like a parable—a story with a hidden meaning? The facts and reality are not always what they seem. Since October 1, 2016, the day of Scott's diagnosis, I feel as though I'm living in a parable. I know the story. I live it daily. I know the characters and plot. What, however, is the meaning? What purpose is there in such physical agony? Why strike down a healthy young man? Why were we asked to watch our son melt away to nothing? I have become like the people of Rome when Pauls describes them as, "without understanding" (Romans 13:1).

Ultimately, I seek the answer to my question, "why?" What is God's will for these days? Why is the death of my son, at such a young age, the will of God? Paul reminds me of truth in this collection of his thoughts, saying, "Consider what I say; and the Lord give thee understanding in all things. . .unto all riches of the full assurance of understanding. . .and to desire that ye might be filled with the knowledge of His will in all wisdom and spiritual understanding" (II Timothy 2:7; Colossians 2:2, 1:9).

The precept that always helps with the *what* and *why*, is found in the classic answer of Jesus to the man who asked what was the greatest commandment (Mark 12:28). After sharing Deuteronomy 6:4–5 with the man, ". . .thou shalt love the Lord thy God with all thy heart. . .," Jesus added the second greatest as well, "Thou shalt love thy neighbour as thyself" (Mark 12:31). The man replied that Jesus had said right, but in his repetition he added a thought, "And to love Him with all thy heart and all thy understanding. . ." (Mark 12:33). Is this not the key? I know God. I believe in God. I know God's Word. But, how much of Him do I understand? "For my thoughts are not your thoughts, neither are your ways my ways, saith the Lord" (Isaiah 55:8). How then do we come to an understanding when the distance between God's thoughts and our thoughts are as vast as the distance between heaven and earth?

As I've mentioned earlier, I compiled some thoughts when I turned forty. Since my son will never reach his full fortieth year, I am re-reading my words to help me now. I wrote an article I called, "An Aroostook County Understanding" at age forty, and I believe it will help me answer my questions in Scott's 40th year:

"At the mere mention of the town Perham, Maine, my imagination soars beyond the countryside, north of the village to a farm rooted deep in the soil of Aroostook County. Though the surrounds were simple, the hospitality was common and freely extended. The love of family and friends carried with it an equal weight for a stranger and close friend. The town, tenants and times molded and shaped my current understandings. For one to understand the meaning of my memories, one must understand the unpretentious people that fashioned my upbringing. You must understand how I was nurtured, and how I grew among the cows and chickens, the oats and potatoes and the hay and clover of the homestead. I realize now that the land fed me, not only physically, but mentally, just as the people fed me spiritually. The influence of the land and its people continue to impact the way I live, the way I work and how I understand what God is doing in my life. Whether writing or preaching, I rest heavily on my understanding of County ways for illustrations and advise. The themes of my past have become the topics of my present occupation. Farm buildings, a big family, country lanes, babbling brooks, fields of golden oats, warm summers, cold winters, sickness and health, fires in the fireplace, homemade bread, and boiled potatoes on the stove all contributed to the practical understanding I now possess. The self-made rich remind me I was raised in poverty. Stuck in the backwoods without the advantages of modern conveniences and isolated from the glitter of city lights, they find me a poor man. But, while the rest of the world gained debt, I gained memories. I experienced things people would give their life savings to enjoy. Oliver Goldsmith once wrote, *"Ill fares the land, to hastening ills a prey, where wealth accumulates, and men decay.*" While the rest of the world grew rich, I became well-versed in the spiritual understanding of what holds value and what does not (Matthew 6:19–21). What most men see as assets, I see as liabilities. I am not impressed by wealth. I prefer health. I am not impressed with possessions. I prefer peace. I am not impressed with fame. I prefer solitude. Only when we get back to the farm philosophy and the soil standards of life will we have the understanding needed to solve the very complicated problems we now face!"

There it is! Within my own thoughts, I found the answer to my current situation. I need to get back to the basic understanding of who God is. It all has to do with "the mind of Christ" (1 Corinthians 2:16). "And we know that the Son of God is come, and hath given us an understanding. . ." (I John 5:20). I believe like Jesus did then, "Then opened He their understanding, that they might understand the Scriptures. . ." (Luke 24:45) He will do so now!

Chapter 20

Quest for Quietness

SOLOMON WROTE A PROFOUND truth when he penned this proverb, "Better is a handful with quietness, than both the hands full with travail and vexation of soul" (Ecclesiastes 4:6). Throughout this travail with Scott's cancer and the vexation his illness has brought into our family, my only relief has been to find a bit of quietness. My thirst for quietness goes back to my upbringing and the quiet days spent on the Blackstone Homestead. When I turned forty, I wrote of the need even then after a visit to see my brother Michael and his family in Pennsylvania.

"I heard this interesting statement recently, "The average person is born in the country, works hard to live in the city, and then he works even harder to get back to the country." After pondering this thought provoking proverb at forty years of age, I feel I can answer the question of why a person would want to get back to a country setting at all cost. I believe the quest to return to the country has everything to do with "quietness."

My brother Michael lives on 'Maine Circle" in Downingtown, Pennsylvania. His home is located in a picture perfect neighborhood, situated on a hillside, nestled in the middle of a forest, just three miles from town. There are nearly one hundred homes in the subdivision. As I glanced at them one morning, during our visit, all I could think was that they'd brought the city to the country. Despite the multitude that lived in that small space, the surrounding hills and trees silenced all the noise from the busy neighborhood. Only the muffled barks of a few dogs and the occasional laughter of children could be heard. Despite being the advertising director for the biggest bank in Delaware, Mike is still a country boy at heart, just like me. Why else would he have Maine Potato bags hanging from his garage walls? He travels an hour in each direction in order to get to work and returns home to his quiet place.

Where can we go for renewal when friends and family fall short or your boss has drained you dry? There is only one place to calm our conscience, restore our reasoning, strengthen our spirit, exalt our expectations, and bolster our bodies. A quiet place beckons us, where all of man is blocked and all of God is brought in. A quiet place where only the sounds of God's natural creation are heard. Only in quietness can we find peace and tranquility. Quietness is the tranquilizer both Mike and I were raised on. We all must make quietness our daily quest!"

The truth of these words ring true again in my life. I find myself drained quickly these days when I fail to find a quiet place. Solomon wrote another proverb on quietness with these lines, "Better is a dry morsel, and quietness therewith, than a house full of sacrifice and strife" (Proverbs 17:1). There has been little strife in our home since our son's illness. He is the ideal patient, rarely complaining and graciously accepting our help. Sometimes, however, we feel as though we are like the three Hebrew children, thrown into a fiery furnace and heated seven times hotter (Daniel 3:19). I am determined to not make the same mistake the children of Israel made, as described by Isaiah, "For thus saith the Lord God, the Holy One of Israel; in returning and rest shall ye be saved; in quietness and in confidence shall be your strength: and ye would not" (Daniel 30:15). The answer is simple: rest and quietness.

Isaiah give another formula for facing life's challenges saying, "And the work of righteousness shall be peace; and the effect of righteousness quietness and assurance for ever" (Isaiah 32:17). Did not God create rest for his crowning creation from the very beginning (Genesis 2:1–2)? Did not God, from the first days of creation, set aside a time to meet and be quiet in the cool of the day (Genesis 3:8)? The Psalmist said it best when he penned, "Be still (or be quiet), and know that I am God. . ." (Psalm 46:10). I believe that rest and quiet, not only come in his presence, but in the simple feeling of his presence. Sometimes even in the midst of great upheavals and trauma one can simply shut their eyes, take a deep breath, and fall into a quiet interlude with the Almighty. There is a great comfort between the knowledge of God's presence and the sense of God's presence, an awareness and consciousness of His presence that brings rest to the soul and quietness to the mind that even cancer cannot destroy.

Paul writes of the greatest instruction on quietness recorded in the Bible when he writes, "That you study to be quiet. . ." (I Thessalonians 4:11). Quietness, like contentment, must be one of the courses a Christian studies in his lifetime (Philippians 4:11). Quietness is not natural, and when coupled with the nature of present difficulties, it can be impossible to find. However, sometimes the best study is not a vacation in a distant place, but learning to have a vacation within, a quiet place internally. My office across the street from our home, in the hour after Scott has been put to bed, has become that place for me. You must build a chapel within yourself where you can go and find rest for your soul; a portable sanctuary in your mind where you go to escape the harsh reality of a dying boy. Jesus might not have had any place to rest His head (Luke 9:58), but we know that He often went to a quiet place to talk with His Dad. Job summarizes my thoughts well saying, "When He giveth quietness, who then can make trouble?" (Job 34:29).

Chapter 21

In the Midst of a Storm

Amid one's lifetime, you will encounter a variety of storms. More often than not, the word "storm" indicates the storms of nature, lightening, wind, snow, or rain storms. There are, however, other kinds of storms like, mental, emotional, business, physical, or family storms. Without a doubt, my family and I are in a cancer storm. I am compiling this chapter just two hours after Hospices' second visit to our home. We signed paperwork today, placing our son under their direct care. We have entered the final weeks of our cancer storm. This is our reality. I return to the words I wrote when I turned forty for comfort:

"My forty year old world hit pause today. The first nor'easter of the New Year blanketed my world, closing schools, cancelling basketball games and shutting me up in my study at the Emmanuel Baptist Church in Ellsworth, Maine. This pause has been the best thing to happen to me in weeks. I love when the good Lord decides to bring things to a screaming halt. Living in a world just short of bewildering bedlam, I am thankful for every pause that occurs. Pause brings a time to ponder and meditate on what has happened and is happening in life. In a world where we are constantly being bombarded with numerous messages, we need to pause lest we go insane with the conflict of voices. While it is only the fourth day of the year, I have much to pause and ponder over.

Only twelve hours into the New Year, my brother phoned to tell me Grants Dairy would no longer be picking up the milk from the Blackstone Homestead cows. Unless something else can be arranged, a hundred and thirty year family farm will end this year. As I stop to consider the magnitude of the news, I cannot imagine returning to the homestead and not seeing a herd of Holsteins grazing on the hillside by Gramie Glenna's home. I cannot envision returning to the farm and not hearing the mooing of milkers coming from the homestead barn. To go home and see no calves, to not drink Blackstone milk and to not smell fresh cut clover, is too upsetting for me to consider. Yet, I must. I pause in pain.

If the news of no more homestead Holsteins happens, what will be next after the cows? The crops? (It was, just a couple years later!) It seems so tragic that mankind is closing down a family farm, while at the same time millions are starving from a famine holocaust in Africa. It seems unbelievable to me that mankind is too nearsighted to see the need of a family farm in the county, while at the same time to farsighted to think there will never come a time when the cows and crops of that country corner will not be needed again. Our farm has become prey to the symptoms of society, geared toward a bigger is better philosophy. No time remains for pauses or places that pause. The bottom line drives society. We must pause and seriously consider the ripple effect of the actions taken toward our family farm, and others like ours. Our society is afraid of secluded, solitary sanctuaries of silence where cows feed freely in picturesque pastures. We will take a moment to pause and remember and then, we will press on!"

That is good advice for someone in the midst of a storm: pause and press on! One of my favorite stories from the life of Christ is the famous event that took place on the Sea of Galilee, in the midst of a storm. I sailed across that Galilean Lake in 2010 and now have a different perspective on the story. Granted, we encountered no storm on the day we crossed, but seeing the surrounding hills, I understand how the disciples would have quickly been caught by the wind. Interestingly, three of the four Gospels tell this tale. God must have wanted us to pay attention to it! After a busy day of ministry, Jesus and his disciples crossed over to the other side and Jesus fell asleep. Matthew describes the scene saying, ". . .There arose a great tempest. . .but he was asleep. . ." (Matthew 8:24). The suggestion of the other writers was the boat was sinking. The fury of the wind or the frenzy of the waves, however, isn't what woke our Saviour. The fear of His disciples woke him from slumber.

Too often amid the storms of life, we, like Jesus' disciples, focus our eyes on the storm rather than the Savior. I readily admit, I have done this same thing during our cancer storm. I forget that God is the God of weather, every storm, whether natural, physical or spiritual. As we discussed in a previous chapter, Satan might be involved, as He used a mighty wind to kill

Job's children (Job 1:19). Before sin, I believe no destructive storms existed. Storms are simply a part of nature's ruin and man's fall.

Anyone of us will travel on tempestuous seas and face mounting winds and waves that seek to overturn us. Yet in the midst of those storms, the Lord taught us how we ought to be: calm, restful and at peace in the midst of a storm. Isaiah gave us this promise from the Almighty when he wrote, *"When you pass through the waters, I will be with you. . ."* (Isaiah 43:2). Jesus was in the boat, just like He promised to be with us (Matthew 28:20). An old song by Hugh Stowell of the nineteenth century starts with this line, "From every stormy wind that blows, from every swelling tide of woes, there is calm, a sure retreat. . .." That "sure retreat" is described in another classic Church hymn:

> The raging storms may round us beat-a shelter in the time of storm
> We'll never leave our sure retreat-a shelter in the time of storm.
> O Jesus is a Rock in a weary land. . .a shelter in the time of storm.

There are times in our present storm where we only see boisterous winds and boiling waves. Mary A. Baker wrote, "Whether the wrath of the storm-tossed sea, or demons, or men, or whatever it be, no water can swallow the ship where lies the Master of ocean and earth and skies; they all shall sweetly obey My will; peace, be still, peace, be still!" I love the simplicity of the wording of Mark's account of this story. Likely, Peter conveyed his version of the storm to Mark, who wrote, "And there arose a great storm. . .And He arose. . ." (Mark 4:37, 39). Never fear, dear child, when the storm arises, so will the Lord! Have you ever noticed as Stephen was being stoned that he saw the Lord 'standing' (Acts 7:56). In every other mention, the Lord is sitting at the right hand of God, yet he stood to help Stephen in his storm. He will do the same for us!

Chapter 22

Why Not Celebrate Now?

I HAVE NOT BEEN in a celebratory mood lately. As well as my son's illness, my mother-in-law Opal, at ninety-two years of age, is in the hospital. The combination of Scott and Opal has drained my wife and me of any energy and joy we have left. This morning, as I read Vance Havner's book *In the Valley of the Shadow of Death* it reminded me:

"When we are passing through great trials and testing we are inclined to wait until the storm is over and the battle ended before we celebrate victory. We lift our weary and tear-dimmed eyes to some blessed day ahead or to heaven itself and sigh for ultimate deliverance. We plod along through gloomy days and desolate nights looking for light at the end of the tunnel. Today is just another dark chapter to be endured."

Havner wrote these words during a day caring for his wife, who had Cushing disease. His conclusion challenged me. He says, "But to the Christian, V-Day (victory day) can be today, no matter what the circumstances are. '. . .this is the victory that overcometh the world, even our faith' (I John 5:4). Our victory was won at Calvary and the open grave. Our Waterloo is behind us and we are engaged only in mopping-up operations!" Thank you, Vance!

After reading this fellow traveller's words, I remember what the Apostle Paul wrote to the Church at Thessalonica, "In everything *(including Scott's sickness and Opal's illness)* give thanks: for this is the will of God in Christ Jesus concerning you" (I Thessalonians 5:18). A few chapters ago, I wrote about my desire to understand the will of God amid this trial. I believe I have found my answer. I may never know the *what* or the *why,* however, I can know the *will*—in everything give thanks! Our victory over these demonic onslaughts is already determined, "But thanks are to God, which giveth us the victory through our Lord Jesus Christ" (I Corinthians 15:57). At the height of the battle, in the midst of the storm, we must not await the end, even when it is out of sight. We can, by faith, triumph in Christ *now,* "Now thanks be unto God, which always causeth us to triumph in Christ. . ." (II Corinthians 2:14). If victory is assured in Christ, why can't we celebrate now?

Havner continues to write what I believe to be true:

"I am passing now through a time of great trial. I do not know what the outcome will be. I do not know when the clouds will lift and the burden fall. I am not merely trying to hold out until then. Today can be a triumph as great and maybe even greater then when the storm abates and the battle ends. I stand in Christ complete. The full and final realization of His triumph has not yet come. We see not yet all things put under Him but we see Jesus and in Him everything is as good as done. This is the victory! There is no doubt as to the outcome. Sin, death, and the Devil are still here, disease and disaster, heartbreak and bereavement is with us but they are defeated foes and we have but to wait a little while to see them all forever past."

What a hope and reassurance these words provide me as I face another day of watching death eat away the frail frame of my warrior boy. His feet are swelling. His eyes are yellowing. His skin is flaking. His breath is more deliberate. He walks like a drunkard. His voice is low and laboring. In the face of this defeat, I can rejoice with the victors, not the victims of cancer. For in Scott's death, he will rise to greater heights and will catch a glimpse of glory bright.

Havner's continued thoughts bring me additional comfort when he writes:

"The Christian belongs to the Kingdom of the Heart, an invisible world at present, but one day it will be set up visibly right here on earth. Meanwhile we taste even now the powers of that age to come and enjoy a foretaste of glory before the King returns. To move through this world as a citizen of heaven is victory now. Principalities and powers (Ephesians 6:12) battle us fiercely but greater is He that is in us than he that is in the world (I John 4:4), and by the shield of faith (Ephesians 6:16) we can ward off the fiery darts of the Wicked One. The outcome is sure; there is not a moment's doubt as to how it will all come out. The devil is on the way out, although he may stir up quite a rumpus in his exit."

This is truly how one gets through the darkest days. Is this not, also, how our Lord and Savior Jesus Christ endured his darkest days. "Looking unto Jesus, the author and finisher of our faith; *who for the joy that was set before him endured the cross*, despised the shame, and is set down at the right hand of the throne of God" (Hebrews 12:2). Jesus looked through the defeat and saw the victory of Calvary. Jesus looked beyond the suffering and saw the joy awaiting Him. Jesus looked into the future and saw the triumph His death would bring. I must do the same.

Finally, Vance Havner writes:

"You can end this drab day with celebration if you live it by the faith of the Son of God. We do not have to wait until we see how it will turn out. It has already turned out! This is the marvelous truth of the gospel that we start from victory and work from it. The ultimate outcome merely climaxes what is guaranteed from the start. You do not have to stand on Jordan's stormy banks and cast a wishful eye to a distant Canaan. We are in Beulah Land now. We can shout hallelujah over the potential until we wait for the actual. True, we do not live by feeling but if all things work together for good there ought to be some happiness now! Let us celebrate victory provided in the past, possible in the present, perfected in the future but victory anytime! This is V-Day! Ours is the Victor and we follow in the train of His triumph. All things are ours already and we are Christ's and Christ is God's."

What a thrilling thought and amazing truth! Ours is not a dead hope, fading wish, or dying desire. In Christ, we have real hope. Paul writes of this hope, saying, "For we are saved by hope: but hope that is seen is not hope: for what a man seeth, why doth he yet hope for? But if we hope for that we see not, then do we with patience wait for it" (Romans 8:24–25). Truly, this is our hope, an unseen hope of ultimate victory and complete triumph over the Devil, disease and death itself.

By God's grace, I aim to live in this victory and celebrate today the triumph that is mine and ours. My prayer in sharing my story, as Havner shared his, will be to help others during their journey through the valley of the shadow of death. My confidence in fighting this battle has soared since reading the words of another amid his own ordeal, yet gracious enough to invite others into his journey. Thirty-four years separate our trials (Havner wrote his book in 1973), but the answer is the same for both: celebrate the victory even in the midst of defeat. Celebrate the triumph we have in Christ, even in the midst of a bitter end.

Chapter 23

When the Well Runs Dry

HAVE YOU EVER HEARD the old saying, *"You never miss the water until the well goes dry?"* If you remember your Bible lessons, Jesus tells the story about a beggar named Lazarus and an unnamed rich man who were neighbors (Luke 16:19–31). Both men die, however, Lazarus goes to "paradise," while the rich man goes to "hell." Do you happen to remember what the rich man craved most in the fires of hell? He pleaded, not for a cup of water, but a mere drop (Luke 16:24) of water. The rich man missed water, only when the well had gone dry! On my fortieth birthday, I wrote an article that highlights this concept of loss:

"I was blessed to be raised on a farm with both my parents and grandparents. I developed strong relationships with both, and the lessons they taught me throughout my lifetime are just now, at forty years of age, being understood and appreciated.

Some would ask, "What can you learn on a dairy and potato farm other than hard work?" Granted, there was plenty of hard labor I struggled to endure. From the earliest of age, I completed chores. While friends went home to complete homework, I completed homework and barn work. While friends had summers off to play, I labored on the homestead seven days a week, from five o'clock in the morning until six o'clock in the evening. We picked rocks and hoed potatoes. The temperatures were hot and the humidity even higher. The fact I was just a kid never seemed to enter the mind of Dad or Gramp. We were all required to work long hours to get the job done, whether filling the hayloft or a potato basket.

While my childhood was hard in one respect, I began to miss it when I moved away. When the middle of September rolled around, I became depressed. At first, I couldn't understand why, until my wife suggested that I was homesick for the harvest. And you know, I was! I missed the lessons of the land. Hard work combined cooperation, unity, helpfulness and the sense of accomplishment. What a better sleep than one of the exhausted from hard work? Many years after I'd left the homestead, I returned to pastor a church about twenty miles from the farm. What a thrill when a man from my church asked me to help him harvest his potato crop! The words from Penny Radford Batts rang true, *'My childhood nightmare had become my adult heaven!'* I returned to the soil, this time loving every long, hard moment. The job had become a joy!

Despite the hard work and long hours, I loved the singleness of purpose and the mutual support that comes from the proverb, 'The family that works together grows closer together!' I believe part of why my siblings and I are so close, is because unbeknownst to us, as we labored together to make a living, we bonded together in such a way that distance or different occupations could not separate. We learned the lesson: you don't miss the water until the well runs dry."

I believe the Lord is teaching me this lesson again as we experience my son's sickness. Who of us has not been guilty of taking someone or something or some place for granted? I took my wife for granted until she came down with breast cancer, and for eight months of my life I did the cooking, washing and cleaning around the house, until the Good Lord gave her back to me (Proverbs 5:18). I took my health for granted until I came down with three kidney stones, and for six months I was in and out of the hospital for procedures and intensive care, until the Lord returned my health (3 John 1). I took my sleep for granted until I could no longer sleep and spent weeks with sleepless nights, until the Lord returned my sleep (Psalm 127:2). I took my father-in-law and fishing partner for granted until he was taken from me from liver and lung cancer, and then the Lord gave me a new fishing partner in Mike Hangge. Who of us have not taken our freedoms or country or Christ himself for granted? Praise the Lord, even if we deny Christ or forsake Him, He will never forsake us nor deny us (Hebrews 13:5; II Timothy 2:13)!

If there is one lesson we have learned through Scott's cancer, it is to take nothing for granted. I could fill a book on the calls, visits and cards from those we have taken for granted through the years. I pray I never live long enough to not have the "water" these people have brought me. The prayers and words of encouragement are like Solomon wrote, "As cold waters to a thirsty soul, so is good news from a far country" (Proverbs 25:25). Then, there is God Himself. How often I have taken my Lord for granted, even when at times it seems He has gone silent. Deep down, I believe, as it was once written, *"I believe in the sun when it does not shine. I believe in God when He is silent. I know the sun is up there even on the darkest day. And when darkness veils Jesus lovely face, I rest on His unchanging grace."*

What well is running dry for you? For me, it is the well of my son. I watch his life's strength dry up one drop at a time. I know there is little left. Will I miss him when he is gone? Absolutely! But, I know I have taken my son for granted over the last twenty years. He didn't always do the things I thought he should do, nor have the friends I hoped he would have. He did not have a relationship with his heavenly Father I hoped he would have either, or maybe I never showed him the right Father! Today, until he reaches his heavenly home and I join him later, I choose not to miss the water his life gives me!

Chapter 24

At the Medical Center

OVER THE LAST SIX months, my wife and I have logged thirty-six day and two hundred and forty hours in medical facilities. We have memorized the layouts of the Cape Fear Medical Center in Fayetteville, North Carolina, as well as the Mary Dow Cancer Clinic and the emergency room of Maine Coast Memorial Hospital in Ellsworth, Maine. Despite the formidable array of medicines, machines and medicine, the modern medical profession has been able to do very little for my son, outside keeping him comfortable. I remain impressed at the assortment of drugs and devices mankind has made to fight this incurable disease and their feeble attempt to prolong death. Doctor Manning, Scott's oncologist, has spoken of prolonging life from the first day they told us that death would be end result. The cures have been impressive, but only in the category of making Scott sicker and his illness more intolerable. In a promise to prolong life, Scott's quality of life vanished. Five week ago, Scott looked me in the eye and said, "I'm done, Dad. Take me home." Only God can now determine how much more earthly life my son will live before ushering him into the glorious promise of eternal life.

I have experienced the cure of certain diseases and cancers within my own family and families within my church. The experts remain baffled with Scott's cancer, however, as just when they get one aliment under control, another rears its ugly head. One step forward and ten steps backwards seem to be the pattern. In one of our first conversations with Dr. Manning, he shared the variety of treatments he had used over the last twenty years to treat Scott's cancer. While he was encouraging and hopeful, deep down I knew the odds were stacked against my son. Time has proven him to be right.

Over the last one hundred and sixty-eight days (the day of this writing), I have stood in the examination rooms amidst the men, machines, and medicines of the medical profession in both the States of North Carolina and Maine. We have seen doctors from the military and civilian institutions, all created by man to help sick men get better. Sometimes they help. Sometimes they simply cannot. I believe Scott's doctors have tremendous intelligence and skill in the field of cancer. I believe the nurses at the Mary Dow Cancer Clinic have the expertise and experience needed to assist patients. Regardless of all their abilities, however, they seem helpless against the onslaught raging in my son's frail body. So despite taking my son to all his appointments, sitting with him through dozens of treatments, and visiting him all eighteen days of hospitalization, I never had my hopes on Scott's earthly physicians. Rather, my eyes are firmly and squarely fixed on the greatest Physician of them all—the Lord Jesus Christ. He alone can heal my son without any medicines, machines or methods. He needs no paraphernalia, poking or prodding, no cat scan, X-ray or MRI. All this Physician requires is a single touch or word and my son would be healed.

A day will come when we no longer need the Medical Center. The gigantic cost of buildings and equipment will be unnecessary when the Lord returns. What man must spend so much time and treasure on, the health of the body, will be forever solved by a new and glorious body (Philippians 2:20–21). As I spend hours in these medical facilities, I ponder the question no one wants to ask, "Why hasn't your Great Physician healed your son?"

The answer to that question lies not in whether He could or could not heal. A simple read of the Gospels concludes Jesus could heal, ". . .all manner of sickness. . .all manner of diseases. . ." (Matthew 4:23). Jesus healed, cured and restored many, but not all. One of the best illustrations for this truth is found in the story of the lame man at the gate called "beautiful" (Acts 3:2). Jesus passed by the man on his numerous visits in and out of the Temple, as Scriptures tells us the man laid at the Temple gate daily. Jesus, however, chose not to heal the man. The miraculous healing was left for Peter and John (Acts 3:7). Even after Jesus left this world for glory, He gave powers of healing to the Church. Again, not everyone received healing. Even Paul could not heal himself, despite healing others (2 Corinthians 12:7; Acts 14:8). Jesus did not heal everyone. Peter did not heal everyone. Paul did not heal everyone. The modern physician cannot heal everyone. God does not choose to heal everyone. Questions arise when a loved one does not receive physical earthly healing. Many believe faith is the key, referencing passages like, "And Jesus seeing their faith. . ." (Matthew 9:2), and, "The prayer of faith shall save the sick. . ." (James 5:15). In the end, however, we must conclude it does not always please the Lord to save the sick, heal the illness, rise up the afflicted, and to cure cancer!

We have seen throughout this journey the difference in God's will versus our own. I have come to pray, "Thy will be done," while simultaneously praying, "Heal my son." I wait to see which prayer will be answered. So, as I stand with the doctors and nurses, I whisper a little prayer the Great Physician to guide their hands, grant them wisdom and to do right by my boy. I ask for them to care for him as if he were their own, and to know when it is time to let go and let God finish the process of prolonging life versus prolonging death.

Though nobody, from Doctor Manning to Doctor Brooks, has ever given us a favorable report on the expectation before us, I believe there is another clinic where examinations, diagnoses, and treatments are handled in a different way. The door is always open and the treatment is free. Everyone who enters finds healing and receives a new body, a cancer free body. Should I contract cancer, like my son, I believe I will choose to admit myself into the Celestial Clinic of Heaven and put my case into the hands of the Great Physician.

Chapter 25

Old Fashion Simplicity

WHEN DID LIFE BECOME so complicated? Life becomes more mysterious the older I get. In my youth, I thought I had so many questions. Now, as I have a thirty-nine year old son dying of cancer, I have more unanswered questions than before. These questions will likely only receive answers in the *hereafter* (John 13:7). My son's illness has provoked more questions about the *hereafter*. Do we stay the same age in heaven, as the age when we went to heaven? What will our resurrected bodies really be like? Will we bear the scars of earth? Will we know each other in heaven, as we knew each other on earth? Will life be simpler there?

I would like to share another observation from the book I wrote when I turned forty. Despite the twenty-six years that have passed since I wrote them, little has changed in my quest for a simpler life, and an even simpler death:

"The bond of the Blackstone family was never stronger than the decades of the 1950's and 1960's. Forty years after that era, I believe I have come to an understanding as to why they shared such closeness: simplicity!

Life was simple. While the world began to experience complications, the Blackstone Homestead remained untouched by it all until the 1970's. I experienced nearly twenty years of simplicity, which I have never experienced since. As I reflect on the past, I discover little money is needed to enjoy life. Material things are not required to live a full life. In the rat race to keep up with Hollywood and Madison Avenue, we have lost the simplicity I once knew on the farm; the simplicity of a four-room, eight-grade schoolhouse rather than a multi-floor complex of gadgets and gangs; the simplicity of a sled instead of a snowmobile; the simplicity of a one channel television instead of a 454 channel satellite dish; the simplicity of an evening playing dominos, rather than an evening fighting over which movie to watch; the simplicity of barn chores instead of boredom; the simplicity of homemade instead of store bought; the simplicity of loving parents instead of divorced partners; the simplicity of math and English instead of computers; the simplicity of country lanes instead of traffic intersections, and the simplicity of sunsets instead of street lights, neighborhood friends instead of turf wars, and the simplicity of farm grown vegetables instead of chemically altered crops.

Decades ago, we never dreamed of fancy store-bought gifts, but rather accepted a simple pair of sneakers that my parents could afford. Mama would make a big bowl of popcorn for my sister and I over the stove or fireplace. Even though it took twice the time to cook than a bag of microwave popcorn, it tasted much better! Homemade bread, chocolate cake and apple pies were all made with natural ingredients. Dad would make a simple, crude rifle with his carving knife for a round of Cops and Robbers with the cousins. Simplicity is what this modern decade of 1990 (and what about now) lacks. They claim to have made housework, jobs, school and shopping simpler. "Life is simpler," they say. But, I ask, "If life is so much simpler, why is it so complicated?"

Could I add one more category to these thoughts on simplicity? Death has become complicated. Yesterday, Hospice came to check on Scott. While she was there, the UPS man delivered a packed. I thought it was more medicine from the VA to help Scott cope. (We receive regular deliveries of medicine to help with everything from pain to nausea to appetite.) This particular box contained over a dozen items to help make Scott comfortable in his final days. As the nurse went through the function and dosage of each medication, my wife and I became increasingly overwhelmed. While the nurse never once said these words, her onslaught of data conveyed one truth: death seems to be more complicated than it used to be!

My daughter Marnie has been dealing with the paperwork side of death. As his power of attorney and executor of his estate, she had all his tax paperwork, bills, check stubs, disability checks, etc. sent to her address in California. California is now claiming that Scott's income is taxable in California, despite never working a day in that state. I sent them the eight dollars they claim is theirs for no other reason than I have nothing inside me to fight them. Complications! In a previous chapter, I shared the complications just getting him out of the state of North Carolina. All I wanted to say was, "He's dying. Let him go." Hours of red tape, drug trials, medicine bottle after medicine bottle, hours of listening to a myriad of doctors and nurses explain the ins and outs of death! We are tired of the complications! Why is it so complicated to die?

Scott desires a few days watching the NCAA basketball tournament, a few moments on the front porch breathing spring air, another cast of a fly with his fly rod into his lucky fishing hole, and just a small ride on his Harley. Scott's needs are now simple: moments of as much normal as he can withstand. We shield him from the complications, because it is not his burden to bear, he's bearing enough! But, I fully admit, I ask the Almighty to remove all complications and take him quietly and simply in his sleep? (Which He Did!)

Chapter 26

This World is Not My Home

WHEN YOU SPEND SIGNIFICANT time around a departing loved one, you begin to think more about there than here (2 Timothy 4:6). Your mind begins to ponder the "over there" and "remaining here" verses. I have been thinking a lot of who Scott will see in heaven before me: my two grandfathers (Roy and Carroll), my two grandmothers (Maude and Glenna), my two uncles (Sherwood and Paul), my two cousins (Bob and Lois), and my father (Wendell) and my father-in-law (Stacy). In addition, I have buried over two hundred church members in my time as a pastor. Sometimes I think there are more over there than here, and soon I will have two sons there (Beven Cherith, the son we miscarried and Scott Alexander).

As I think of this "over there" and "remaining here," I like to remind myself of the old church hymn written by Albert E. Brumley, *This World is Not My Home,* sometimes known as, *I'm Just Passing Through.* I have never found the history behind this hymn. I suspect, however, Brumley was enduring something similar to what my family and I are. Let me remind you of the words, if you've never heard them:

> This world is not my home, I'm just passing thru.
> My treasures are laid up somewhere beyond the blue.
> The angels beckon me from heaven's open door,
> And I can't feel at home in this world anymore.

They're all expecting me, and that's one thing I know.
My Saviour pardoned me and now I upward go.
I know He'll take me thru tho I am weak and poor,
And I can't feel at home in this world anymore.

I have a loving mother (son) up in gloryland.
I don't expect to stop until I shake her hand.
She waiting now for me in heavens open door,
And I can't feel at home in this world anymore.

Just up in gloryland we'll live eternally.
The saints on every hand are shouting victory.
Their song of sweetest praise drifts back from heaven's shore,
And I can't feel at home in this world anymore.

O Lord, you know I have no friend like you.
If heaven's not my home then Lord, what will I do?
The angels beckon me from heaven's open door,
And I can't feel at home in this world anymore.

I am homesick for Heaven these days, and have often thought of heaven since I punched my ticket for that celestial land in 1958. When I started in my ministry in 1973, I had the opportunity to write a bit of prose for certain events, sermons, and special occasions. One of my earliest poems was this simple thought:

Heaven is better than this, no more worry, no more fears, no more crying, and no more tears. Yes, heaven is better than this. Heaven is better than this, no more problems, no more pain, no more snow, and no more rain. Yes, heaven is better than this. Heaven is better than this, no more darkness, no more nights, *no more dying*, no more fights. Yes, heaven is better than this!

Why has heaven had such a hold on me since I was the young age of seven? I believe the answer can be summarized in these simple thoughts:

Heaven means *HIM.* Jesus told His earliest disciples: "Let not your heart be troubled: ye believe in God, believe also in me. In my Father's house are many mansions: if it were not so, I would have told you. I go to prepare a place for you. And if I go and prepare a place for you, I will come again and receive you into myself; *that where I am, there ye may be also*" (John 14:1–2).

Another favorite hymn of mine says, "The sky shall unfold preparing His entrance. The stars shall applaud Him with thunders of praise. The sweet light in His eyes shall enhance those awaiting, and we shall behold

HIM then face to face!" I have waited nearly sixty years to see Him. Why would I not want to go?

Heaven means *HAPPINESS*. John wrote in the book of Revelation, "Blessed (or happy) are the dead which die in the Lord from henceforth. . ." (Revelation 14:13). My life has been full of happiness: finding the love of my life, Coleen; the birth of my son and daughter, pastoring four churches covering nearly fifty years, getting my books published, trips to Israel, India and Australia, holding my grandson Judah and granddaughter Elena. I am confident to say with Paul, "Eye hath not seen, nor ear heard, neither have entered into the heart of man, the things which God hath prepared for them that love Him" (I Corinthians 2:9). I believe my greatest happiness is yet before me!

Heaven means *HOME*. The Bible describes the believer as a "stranger and pilgrim" (1 Peter 2:11, Hebrews 11:13–16). Why? This world is not my home! I found this simple poem years ago that continues to bless my heart. It reads, "Along the golden streets, no stranger walks today, but he who long homesick, is home at last to stay!" Do you know and believe the words to this song?

> When engulfed by the terrors of a tempestuous sea;
> Unknown waves before me roll.
> At the end of doubt and peril is eternity,
> Though fear and conflict seize my soul.
> When surrounded by the blackness of the darkest night;
> O how lovely death can be.
> At the end of this long tunnel is a shining light;
> for death is swallowed up in victory.
> But just think of stepping on shore and finding it heaven,
> Of touching a hand and finding it God,
> Of breathing new air and finding it celestial,
> Of waking up in glory and finding it home!

The *Our Daily Bread* published an article I would like to share with you to conclude this chapter. It reads:

> "The 18th century English pastor Rowland Hill lived to a ripe old age. In fact, he outlived most of his friends. Missing them very much and anxious to join them on the other side, he grew more homesick for heaven with each passing day. It seemed so long since some of them had gone to glory that he would often jokingly say with a wink, 'Do you think they'll remember me?' It was not unusual for him to go to some other believer well along in years with this request: 'If you should go before I do, give my

love to everyone. Be sure to tell them that old Rowley, although staying behind a little while, is coming on as fast as he can.' C. H. Spurgeon, commenting on death for the Christian, observed that it's wonderful to ". . .have the tenement gradually taken down, and yet not to feel any trouble about it, but to know that you are in the great Father's hands, and you shall wake up where old age and infirmities will all have passed away, and where, in everlasting youth, you shall behold the face of Him you love.'" Amen and Amen!

Chapter 27

Heavenly Handshake

AFTER WRITING MY LAST chapter, I continued to think about my son Scott travelling toward heaven. I believe he has entered heaven's borderland. I know he has the natural fears that most have regarding the transition from here to there. I try to encourage him, however, there is nothing to fear. Just last night as I put him to bed (a strange thing to do with your thirty-nine year old son), we talked of letting go and slipping into the hands of God. I believe when the time comes, it will happen in "the twinkling of an eye" (1 Corinthians 15:52). When Scott arrives on the shore of eternity, all his questions will disappear and the ecstasy of eternity will cause everything from earth to dissolve. Vance Havner once wrote, *"The dearest things here will be dearer there."*

A few years ago, I found a poem by Dennis Swanberg entitled, *I Just Got to Thinking How Beautiful Heaven Is."* I repeated "amen!" after each line. It reads like this:

> I just got to thinking how beautiful heaven is.
> It is the sweet home of the happy and free.
> It is the fair haven of rest for the weary.
> It is a beautiful, beautiful place.
> When I picture heaven and I quite often do.
> I may not think of the things that mean the most to you.
> Like jasper walls or gates of pearl, so beautiful to behold, or mansions standing everywhere on streets of solid gold.
> For that is not what appeals to me, nor fills my heart with bliss

Because I have never had enough of these to miss.
I guess the human mind can't comprehend the beauty there to see,
But this my friend is what heaven means to me.
It is a place where night will have vanished away,
And the age of time will be one long day.
The weather will be perfect and food will be fine.
And we will never have to hurry because there will be no more time.
And there in heaven we won't ever cry and there will be no bills to pay,
Because there will be nothing to buy.
There will be no more sorrow, not one bit of sin,
And the sting of death will never be felt again.
Another thing to me that will make heaven so fair,
For my mum and dad will both be there.
And looking so young and fair to me,
Not old and wrinkled like they used to be.
I want to kiss my mum and hear her whisper in my ear,
`` I've been waiting for you, and I am so glad you're here.'
And daddy will say, 'There is no more fears'
And we'll sit down and just talk, for maybe a hundred years.
Try to imagine the thrill of seeing old saints and shaking their hands
And hearing all the stories of the things they have done,
And maybe live right next door to old James and John!
It's going to be wonderful,
If we make it through to this beautiful land He's made for me and for
you. But all that I've mentioned will not even be compared,
To the main thrill that awaits us when we get up there.
That's to see Jesus who died for me,
And to live in His presence throughout all eternity.
I'll just sing forever without a trouble or a care,
That's what heaven means to me and I sure hope I'll meet you there!"

Dennis makes mention in his beautiful lines about the saints and of "shaking their hands." His words reminded me of another observation I made about my grandfather's handshake when I turned forty. One of the people waiting for my son on the shores of heaven is his great-grandfather, Carroll Blackstone. Gramp Carroll was my childhood mentor and inspiration, and as a result we were quite close. He made an earlier trip to gloryland than I would have wanted, dying in 1975. One of my first heavenly appointments, after seeing my Savior of course, will be to find Carroll and shake his hand as we did in my boyhood. (Interestingly, one of the very first articles I ever had published was called "Grandpa's Handshake." The Country Extra Magazine published it in the September 1998 edition, and reprinted the piece in 2005 for their "The Best of Country" feature.) I wrote this in 1991:

"When I remember my Grandfather Blackstone, I recall his hands. I can see Gramp now carrying a bale of hay in each hand down the length of the car barn to a stall of young yearling in the back of the barn. I see again in my mind's eye those powerful hands wrapped around the teats of a Holstein's udder as he filled a pail with milk. His hands were sure and fast as he changed the milking machines from one cow to another. How often those hands assisted me as I help with the chores I know not, but this I will never forget at forty, the assurance of a grandfather's handshake!

When you're young and put your hand into the hand of a man to settle a deal, it does something to you. I still have fond memories of the day Gramp removed his right-hand glove and extended his huge-paw to me and said for the first time, 'We got a deal!' I had just been hired on to help Gramp pick rocks for a dollar a day. I learned quickly that a handshake was no trivial thing. To Gramp a handshake was a sacred oath, bathed in honor and integrity. He not only expected you to keep your end of the bargain, but he was determined that he would keep his. Whether that first day job deal or the $1500 I borrowed from him to buy my first home, each was signed with a handshake, not a pen! His handshake was as good as his word, and though his grip swallowed mine on that first day of work, a crisp one dollar bill was deposited in my hand at the end of that day.

We made many other deals during my boyhood. I recalled another today, having recently been home to the homestead to see my sickly grandmother, Gramp's wife of over 50 years. Despite the fact that she has outlived him by nearly 20 years (Glenna would eventually live into her one hundredth year), hardly a meeting goes by we don't speak of Gramp. A few days ago our conversation came around to the days I use to mow Gramp's lawn. Gramie reminded me of the day when Gramp thought I had gotten old enough to be responsible for his lawn and yard. Gramp took great pride in the appearance of his home (a house I owned for nine year), and I didn't realize until years later just how much of an honor it was to be given that responsibility. Once again the deal was sealed with a handshake. My hands had grown by that time, but once again his hand swallowed mine. For the three hour job I got three dollars, quite a raise. When I mentioned that the other day to Gramie, she did remind me of the perks I also received. Halfway through each mowing, Gramie would come out and invite me into the house. Setting on the table was a few cookies and a bottle of Orange Crush soda, my favorite as a child.

Today, a handshake means nothing. All transactions must be in black and white, witnessed, notarized, and then most are not binding. Now that I have reached adulthood, I have a new appreciation of Gramp's handshake.

Carroll Blackstone's handshake signified a pledge and was as good as the hand that shook on it."

Oh, to feel that big hand in mine one more time! I believe I have one more handshake to share with my Gramp: a heavenly handshake on the shores of heaven.

Chapter 28

Battling Insomnia

ONE OF THE TRAUMAS to attack my wife and me through this battle with cancer is insomnia. I thought we would be so exhausted from constant care sleep would come regardless. How wrong I was! Today marks day one hundred and seventy-three and last night proved again how trying insomnia can get. My wife and I are attacking this evil in two different ways. Coleen sleeps whenever she can, day or night, to fight the exhaustion. I, on the other hand, have tried to keep a routine, early to bed, but not too early to rise and resisting the urge to nap during the day. Last night, I went to bed at 9:30 p.m. and read for an hour, as usual. However, when Scott stirred at 2:30 a.m., so was I. Scott had gone to bed upstairs tonight, rather than staying downstairs to sleep in his chair. With his tremendous weight loss and aching all over from the growing tumors, Scott finds his recliner to be more comfortable. Once I got Scott settled back downstairs at 3:00 a.m., sleep escaped me.

Insomnia is a common complaint as I read the accounts of others travelling through this valley of the shadow of death. The prospect of loneliness and separation and painful dying has caused scores of caregiver's sleepless nights of agonizing sorrow. The unknowns of tomorrow's uncertainties have chased sleep away, as the mind tosses and turns night after night thinking through all that might happen, could happen, and will happen. The need to keep a sharp ear opened to the slightest call or strange noise. I know this is what aroused me out of a deep sleep last night. The simple noise of my son's feet shuffling across the carpet from his bedroom to the bathroom. Scott can no longer really walk due to how weak he is. His feet can only rise enough to shuffle on the floor.

Insomnia can be looked at two different ways. Chronic insomnia can be a device of the devil (2 Corinthians 2:11), in order to keep the saint tired, irritable, unproductive and not functioning in the ministry of the Lord. Some of God's best servants have battled this scourge for parts of their lives. I have read the accounts of men like Vance Havner, R.A. Torrey, and others who describe the sleepless nights, despite counting sheep and reading till the dawn. I believe it is an affliction that attacks many. I have discovered, however, that this is not the kind of insomnia my wife and I face now. What is happening, then? Is there an answer to why insomnia has hit us now? What can be done to change it? What did the people of the Bible do when insomnia hit them (i.e. King Ahasuerus, Esther 6:1; King Darius, Daniel 6:18)?

A simple look into my concordance reveals the Bible speaks a lot about sleep, but not insomnia specifically. I have come to believe, however, that insomnia is implied in the verses I will share with you. I love the story of an old bishop who struggled to sleep one night. As he lay in bed, eyes wide open, he grabbed his Bible and read, "Behold, He that keepeth Israel shall neither slumber nor sleep" (Psalm 121:4). His conclusion was simple and recorded his epiphany, "Well, Lord, if you are sitting up there is no sense in my doing it. Goodnight, Lord!"

My favorite verse on the subject is Psalms 127:2 which states, "It is vain for you to rise up early, to sit up late, to eat the bread of sorrow: for *He giveth His beloved sleep!*" I discover that with each and every battle with insomnia, I eat the bread of sorrow. After getting Scott settled last night, I fell into a deep sorrow. Sorry for his suffering and the one lying beside me in bed and all she is enduring, as well. Coleen bears a double portion of sorrow, as her mother endures from a number of chronic illnesses. In the nearly twelve years Opal has lived near us, not a winter passes where she is not hospitalized. This winter, the winter of Scott's cancer, she had been doing so well. Just a few days before spring, however, she ended up in the hospital. Over the last eight days, Coleen has been bouncing between hospital care of her mother and home care with her son. She came home last night from visiting her mother and collapsed in full fatigue.

This morning I recognized that sometimes insomnia is allowed by the Almighty to teach us a greater lesson. Last night as I ate the bread of sorrow, I prayed. I prayed God would take this sorrow of Coleen's mother away, not in death, but a simple solution. I just returned from checking on my charge across the road, and my wife greeted me with wonder news. Overnight, Opal thought through her situation and decided the best way she could help her daughter was to voluntarily go to the rehab center, as recommended by the doctors, rather than fighting to live on her own. We are so grateful for this miracle!

I have no easy, glib magic spell for your insomnia. I suggest, however, that if you cannot sleep, supplicate instead. Paul and Silas should have been so exhausted after their beating and trial that they fell into a deep sleep. Just the opposite occurred! Even amid their shackles, they spent the night in praise and prayer (Acts 16:25). Remember, God knows our frame and He knows we need sleep. But, sometimes He allows insomnia so He can talk to us and we can talk to Him.

If your mind is too tired to think of something to pray about, consider this verse, "When thou liest down, thou shalt not be afraid" yea, thou shalt lie down, and they sleep shall be sweet" (Proverbs 3:24). The Lord provides sweet sleep that a bottle of tranquilizers cannot give. Pills have a place, and are needed at times. I would never deny my son the sleeping pills given by the doctor to help him survive the agonizing suffering he endures. I have also prescribed to him the wonderful God-assisted sleep that comes by simply resting in Him. David writes, "I laid me down and slept; I awoke; for the Lord sustained me" (Psalm 3:5). David writes again, "I will both lay me down in peace, and sleep: for thou, Lord, only makest me dwell in safety" (Psalm 4:8).

Sleep comes from the Lord. Sleep is a wonderful gift from the heavenly Father to His children. When it is taken from us, we must go to Him first, seek the reason and when an answer is given, lie back and drift into the slumber He provides.

Chapter 29

A Land of Unclouded Days

BY MY VERY NATURE, I love watching clouds. I like to know what the weather will be and when it will come. I like watching the weather. I think this stems from my upbringing on a working potato and dairy farm in Northern Maine. The weather was vital to all we did. I still remember this precept my father taught me from the Bible about weather. Ecclesiastes 11:4 says, "He that observes the wind shall not sow; and he that regardeth the clouds shall not reap." Perhaps it was then that I first became an observer of the clouds. A cloudy day isn't necessarily a bad day. I would rather fish on a cloudy day with wind and rain, than a cloudless one. I have caught more trout on a cloudy day than a bright, blue sky kind of day! During my trips to India, I enjoy the cloudy day over the cloudless one, because of the shade the clouds provide. Days where the temperature rises to over hundred degrees are common. The shade of clouds feels glorious!

The Lord gave me insight into the purposes of clouds one day while reading about the children of Israel's and their wilderness wanderings. Psalm 121:5–6 reads, "The Lord is thy keeper: the Lord is *thy shade* upon thy right hand. The sun shall not smite thee by day, nor the moon by night." During a visit to Israel, I understood that any shade on a sunny day is better than no shade at all! There is an old church hymn that suggests heaven will be "a land of unclouded days." What could the writer mean by that phrase?" Here are the words to the song:

Oh, they tell me of a home beyond the skies;
Oh, they tell me of a home far away.
Oh, they tell me of a home where no storm clouds rise;
Oh, they tell me of an unclouded day.

Oh, they tell me of a home where my friends have gone;
Oh, they tell me of that land far away.
Where the Tree of Life in eternal bloom,
Sheds its fragrance through an unclouded day.

Oh, they tell me of a King in His beauty there,
And they tell me that my eye shall behold.
Where He sits on the throne that is whiter than snow,
In the city that is made of gold.

Oh, they tell me that He smiles on His children there,
And His smile drives the sorrows away.
And they tell me that no tears ever come again,
In that lovely land of unclouded day.

Oh, the land of cloudless day.
Oh, the land of an unclouded day.
Oh, they tell me of a home where no storm clouds rise.
Oh, they tell me of an unclouded day.

A simple look into the Word of God and you will discover these things about clouds. The prophet Nahum tells us that clouds are the dust on God's feet (Nahum 1:3). The Almighty created the clouds above (Proverbs 8:28). God creates a cloudy day (Psalm 147:8). One day, the Lord will come back in the clouds just like He left in the clouds (Acts 1:9; Revelation 1:7). David talked of a cloudless day when he penned, "And He shall be as the light of the morning, when the sun riseth, even a morning without clouds; as the tender grass springing out of the earth by clear shining after rain" (II Samuel 23:4). David linked God with an unclouded day!

A few years back I prepared a series of sermons related to the theme of being homesick for heaven. I captioned one sermon in particular, "A Prepared Place." I quoted Vance Havner who said, *"The curtain between here and hereafter grows thin as we await the parting of the veil."* The great gathering of the church is near (1 Thessalonians 4:13–18), and we must know as much about our heavenly home as we can. I shared these three concepts. Heaven is a *country* (Hebrews 11:13–16) and our *citizenship* is there, not here (Ephesians 2:19). I am a citizen of the greatest country in the world, but I, like Abraham, am looking for a heavenly country. Heaven has a *city* (Hebrews 11:10, 16), a God-planned, God-built city beyond our dreams (I Corinthians 1:9; Revelation 21:10–21). Heaven contains *crowns* (I Peter 1:3–4), a place where we shall receive our inheritance, our reward and our crowns (James 1:12 and I Peter 5:4). Heaven is a prepared place for a prepared people (Romans 13:12). Vance Havner also said, *"A place where all question marks will be straightened up into exclamation points!"* Should I add a fourth point to that sermon, heaven has only *cloudless* days?

As I ponder this concept, in the light of my son Scott, I realize, unlike me, Scott loves cloudless days. Scott choose, after eight years in the ARMY, to settle in North Carolina, a place with a significant more amount of cloudless days than Maine, not to mention cloudless winter days are much warmer in North Carolina! If darkness is going to disappear from heaven, why not cloudy days as well (Revelation 21:25)? Could the imagery be as simple as the unbroken fellowship with the Almighty? As an unclouded day does not hinder a cloudless sky, there is nothing to block the Son from shining (Revelation 21:23). I realized for the last six months my family has been living under a dark, gloomy canopy of cancer. We have shared a few bright days since Scott's diagnosis of neuroendocrine carcinoma. Like a polluted cloudy day, the weather has not only been dreary, but hazy. We have yet to see clearly through all that is happening. The old saying, "On a clear day, you can see forever," has yet to be true for us. As I ponder more on the place my son is journeying towards, I believe the days for him will become clearer, brighter and cloudless!

From Scott's bedroom and the living room where he sits in his favorite recliner, he can see the steeple of the Emmanuel Baptist Church, his home church. As the raging cancer consumes his flesh, my prayer is that he looks out the window to the white steeple and sees a directional signal to a place of cloudless days. In the darkest days here, he will see that steeple pointing to a better world, a world of perfect weather. I pray he is ready to join the saints above, and walk with them on streets of gold under an unclouded day. Where once he struggled through the worst storm of his life, he will stretch his new legs under the kind of sky he loved to play golf under—cloudless!

Today, as I wrote this chapter, a snow squall came through town. The air is wintry again, even though a friend of mine said he saw a flock of robins in town! The weather mirrors the climate Scott endures; and the earthly weatherman is forecasting a final assault of winter in this first week of spring. The medical weatherman has also predicted many a dark, painful day ahead for Scott. The old adage that it gets darker before it gets brighter applies now. There is a day coming, however, when the forecast will always be of a cloudless day!

My wife and I are not optimistic or pessimistic about what we face with our son; we are realists. We see things as they are, as seemingly as God has wanted them. But like John of old in his dark prison of Patmos, we are not looking for 'a pie in the sky.' We look for an unclouded day, when we will walk with our son again in full health and full strength in a 'glorified body' (Philippians 3:20). The Apostle John has become my favorite weatherman, and I am resting in his forecast of a land of unclouded days!

Chapter 30

Awaiting the Outcome

I HAD FINALLY FALLEN asleep after hours of tossing and turning and thinking and praying about our dear son, when I heard, "Barry! I need you!" Waking suddenly, I found myself disoriented, especially at 4:30 a.m. I rushed downstairs to find my son sitting on the floor between the dining room and living room. Over the last week, we transformed the living room into his bedroom and dining room into his bathroom. The distance between the two room's spans ten feet, the height of a basketball hoop, a hoop my son once could score at ease, but now struggles to shuffle across. Trying to return to his recliner (his new bed), Scott lost his balance and fell, hurting his shoulder -the shoulder that once made all those baskets. Once so stable and balanced to sink every three-pointer, foul shot or layup, he staggers like an old man of ninety, not forty. His mother and I lifted him to his chair, knowing this is just one small event of many to come as we await the final outcome.

On October 20, 2016, Scott was admitted into Cape Fear Hospital in Fayetteville, North Carolina complaining of severe pain in his liver. On October 25, 2016 (exactly five months ago from the time of this writing), he was diagnosed with a small cell cancer called Neuroendocrine Carcinoma, a deadly, rapid moving cancer that usually takes its victim within eight months. For the first three weeks, Scott suffered from the pain and the chemotherapy, but made enough of a comeback to travel home to Maine by plane. Scott no longer wished to stay in his adopted state of North Carolina, but wanted to return to his home state of Maine to continue treatment and recovery. Over the next few months, Scott's condition relapsed several times, forcing us to take him to our local hospital (Maine Coast Memorial Hospital). Attached to this medical center is the Mary Dow Cancer Clinic where Scott received five rounds of treatment. The final two treatments destroyed what little health Scott had, and once again he was admitted into the hospital for a five day period we thought would be his last. (His attending doctor told us on February 16, Scott would live only a few days. Little did she know my son will live forever!) Scott took a turn for the better and we were able to bring him back home. My wife and I marvel that he is still with us and thank God for a glimmer of hope! This morning as we pulled him off the floor, our hope faded as we realized one again we are simply waiting for the final outcome.

I desire you as the reader to know that Scott has received the best of care during each phase of this journey. The doctors and nurses attending to him have given their best. We knew, however, early on that this cancer was beyond their medical expertise, medicines, and machines. They had come face to face with a disease that ultimately only the Good Lord could heal, if He chose that path! By "healing," I am referring to a physical healing. We see now Scott will receive only an eternal healing, one that seems just days away from occurring.

Actually, for the first time since this terrible journey began I heard Scott's mother say she didn't want to see him suffer anymore. When you have to pick your son off the floor as you once did when he stumbled learning to walk, it changes your focus when you pick him up in the same manner, but he's only thirty-nine. We have no illusions about what some call "faith healings." We have pet peeves on why some are healed and some are not. But our original hope was that God would choose to heal him from this disease, as a miraculous testimony of His power over man's procedures. Does God still work miracles? My mother-in-law's willingness to give up driving and allow herself to be put into a rehab center for two weeks are two miracles we have witnessed over the last few days! But God chooses in His divine providence when and who such healing miracles are administered. I believe it should not be an odd event when the Great Physician hears our prayers, heeds our requests, and heals our loved ones. It should also not be a strange thing when He does not! Ours is but to await the outcome.

No matter how much time remains, or how it will all end for my son this side of eternity, there is one thing my wife, my daughter, and I are determined to do as we wait—glorify the Lord. I learned this precept from the pen of the Apostle Paul years ago. He writes, "Whether therefore ye eat, or drink, or whatsoever ye do (or wait on the departure of a loved one), do all to the glory of God" (I Corinthians 10:31). We are confident that somehow, someway our Lord and Saviour Jesus Christ will find a way to get glory out of this waiting period. For some, this seems like an irreconcilable dilemma, the sovereign will of God verses the free will of man. The Gospel of John teaches that we can ask anything and God will allow it (15:7, 5:14). Most, however, forget to apply the concept of 1 John 5:14 which states, "And this is the confidence that we have in Him, that, *if we ask anything according to His will*, He heareth us!" We must understand these principles together, and where there seems to be conflict we must allow the Almighty to harmonize them into His perfect will. In the end, I believe that His will, not mine, will be the better will. Our responsibility in all this is too simply await the outcome!

Just over a year and a half ago, I worried how I would properly teach the book of Job. Little did I know the Good Lord would bring about this cancer journey as a firsthand experience of watching another Job loss everything. While Scott didn't have as much as Job, they share a loss of health and wealth in common. Together, they are sick beyond belief, enduring pain, discomfort beyond imagination (Job 2:8), being watched by family (2:9) and friends (2:11). When the Scriptures become that personal, you have a different perspective on the meaning of the message of the Word of God. I challenge you to be sincere when you ask for new insight into God's Word (Luke 11:1) or desire to be conformed into the image of Christ (Romans 8:29). God might just teach you what you want through your own trial of cancer or another's trial.

From the beginning, I have prayed that I might take this burden from my son. Perhaps someday my own cancer will come. But after this morning, I am convinced again that it is much harder to pick someone else up from the floor than allow someone else to pick you up. We all want to learn something from God through the delightful, wonderful life experiences. But, as we know from stories like Job, God uses even the difficult experiences of life to teach us. There are just some things God can only teach us in the dark. And we are in the dark as we await the outcome.

As I wait, I am reminded of a saying by the famous American William Jennings Bryan who says, "*Christ has made of death a narrow starlit strip between the companionship of yesterday and the reunion of tomorrow!*" If I know my theology, and I believe I do, the outcome will be glory for son and grief for us. Our grief will only be temporary. We have the blessed hope that the family of God is not really divided, but one family here and one family there; like Marnie in California and me in Maine. So we await the verdict, the decision, the outcome; and as for me and my family we proclaim, "To God be the Glory!"

Chapter 31

Getting an Education

WHEN I WAS A boy, the bulk of my education came from three places, the Perham Elementary School, the Blackstone Homestead and the First Baptist Church of Perham. At forty, I wrote down my philosophy of education based on what I learned from these places.

"There are two ways to learn about any subject, education or example! (I would now add a third to my list, experience.) In the informational age of the 1990's, we have redefined education to mean the learning of information. We have a lot of people in our society with a head full of facts, but still unemployed. They know dates, theories, and historical facts, but they have not the wherewithal to land or hold onto a job. While the younger generation knows more about their world than their parents did at their age, they remain ill mannered, foul speaking, and awkward in their social skills. They have received most of their information through television, music and the computer with few having had a genuine human being as a teacher. When will we relearn that information is not education?

I learned the three R's at our four-room, eight-grade rural elementary school where the education was anything but elementary, and man, not machine, gave me my education. What I didn't learn at Perham Elementary, I learned through the examples of godly parents, grandparents, aunts, and uncles on the homestead and righteous men and women at church. We can now buy books on just about any subject matter imaginable. We can read those books and discover the in's and out's about any subject. We can learn rules, regulations and restrictions. Until we can put those teachings into practice and discover their assets and liabilities for ourselves, we have been informed but not educated. Applying methods of learning is a far better way! Mixing education and example will allow us to learn how to apply the facts we learned. This was the method from the Perham Elementary School teachers of my boyhood. We didn't have much in the way of equipment, but we had plenty of positive examples in the staff at the school. Learning was a life skill taught day in and day out, inside and outside the school building.

If all we learn is the cold, hard facts, we will fall short in our training to one day teach or work in an occupation. To study history is one thing, but until you have a teacher like Mr. Harper who lived history, you will have no real knowledge of history. To play baseball correctly takes practice and repetition, but to catch the ball and hit the ball takes a Coach like Woody Doody to show you the right way. There are just some things that can't be learned in books; these are matters for the heart, not the head. The best way to learn anything is to get involved. Stop studying it, analyzing it, and start dreaming it, and living it. Take what you have in your head and put it into your hand. Experience firsthand what you read about in your textbook. Only then will your skills in a certain field really come to light.

I have known individuals who have gone to school for years studying a particular subject only to discover when they finally began to work in their chosen field they have no deep seeded desire to do it for the rest of their lives. Why are our community colleges full of people seeking training in a secondary field? Most attend because unlike me at forty, they never learned in a small-country school, a small-country church, and on a small family farm that information is not education!"

The truths of yesterday apply to today. Oh the education Coleen and I are receiving while caring for a dying loved one! After nearly forty-four years in ministry, one would assume I know a fair amount about death and dying. However, my education is now hands-on experience. I used to drift in and out as I minister to individuals and families as their loved ones passed. I thought I had a good education in what to say, what to share. Sometimes you need to just be there and keep still. I never wanted to be a "Job's comforter" (Job 2:11–13). I honed my skills over the years. Each situation with cancer helped me understand and become more knowledgeable about one of man's greatest scourges. I thought I had adapted well and knew how to serve the sick, revive the downhearted and comfort the caregiver. Needless to say, I know differently now. I had much to learn.

The Lord created me for ministry by giving me the ability to not get caught up in the trauma, and not become weighted down with the difficulties my parishioners experienced. When I left the hospital or home, I left the burden there. After I visited the shut-in, shut-out or shut-away, I left them in the hands of God and carried on with my day. What I never learned, in all those encounters for nearly half a century, is the intense, up close, firsthand, traumatic education that comes with the patient, parishioner and person is your own son. I had read the books, pamphlets and articles on all this. I thought I had a good head knowledge facing this journey. But, I am learning that information might be good for the head, but it is useless for the heart.

I just returned from checking on my son across the street. I stood over his sleeping form and counted his breaths. I learned this from a nurse when we believed Scott would die a few weeks ago. Shallow breathing is a sign of coming death. As I counted only six breaths (sixteen is normal) in one minute, I realized what this dear nurse, who is also a parishioner of mine, told me in hopes to help me understand the stage Scott is in. Knowledge is powerful if applied. Knowledge helps us understand where we are and where we are going. Truth, even medical truth, is forever a scaffold that helps us hold up when we seemingly have nothing to hold on too. That is why I am determined to apply the Biblical education I have received over the years to my son's case. Death seems to be winning today. But my Savior said this, "I am the resurrection, and the life: he that believeth in me, though he were dead (or dying), yet shall he live: and whosoever liveth and believeth in me shall never die. Believeth thou this?" (John 11:25–26). I believe! From the earliest days of my youth, I have believed that Jesus Christ conquered death for days just like today. When my son departs, I believe he will be more alive than he is today!

As we approach the final days of my son's life on earth, I rest in the teachings of the Word of God, and the specific truth, ". . .the former things are passed away" (Revelation 21:4). There is a day coming when God will "make all things new" (Revelation 21:5). I am educated in the hereafter and it is time for me to apply that education to my son. I believe my son will be in heaven the moment he breathes his last breath (2 Corinthians 5:8). I believe he will be with family the minute he reaches gloryland (Ephesians 3:15). I believe he will enter heaven because he has done what the Bible tells us needs to be done (John 14:6), and I believe he will be there when I arrive either through the rapture (I Thessalonians 4:16), or my own departure from earth. These truths are the comfort of my spiritual education as I face the cruelest of cancers (1 Thessalonians 4:18). Today, things are a mess, but, there is a day coming when all things will be made right (1 Corinthians 14:40). Today, I long for that day.

Chapter 32

Beyond the Blue

A FEW CHAPTERS BACK, I shared my favorite song about heaven with you, "This World Is Not My Home." In that hymn, there is a phrase that says, "my treasures are laid up somewhere beyond the blue." The more I ponder and meditate on what my son endures, the more my mind drifts to life "beyond the blue."

An anonymous poet once penned, "Passing beyond the shadow into a purer light. Stepping behind a curtain, getting a clearer sight; passing out of the shadow into eternal day; why do we call it dying: this sweet going away?" In a book called, The Three Deadly Foes, Henry Durbanville shares this story:

"At dusk, a little girl entered a cemetery. An old man who sat at the gate said to her, "Aren't you afraid to go through the cemetery in the dark?" "Oh, no," she replied, "My home is just on the other side!"

What a wonderful way for anyone nearing their final resting place on earth to see death. Being in the pastorate for nearly forty-four years, I have had ample opportunity to spend a lot of time in cemeteries. One of the things I enjoy doing while I wait for a committal service to start, is to wander around and read the inscriptions on the tombstones. I have noticed that people today rarely put an inscription on the side of their loved one's gravestone. Years ago, however, it was common practice. I like this one, "Gone Home with a Friend!" The departing of a Christian is a kind of homegoing, and for some of us we long for our turn. Yes, I truly at times envy my son. Granted, I do not envy what he has endured to go home to heaven.

But, I am like the missionary that was caught up in the Boxer Rebellion in China at the beginning of the twentieth century. This missionary came the closest one can come to martyrdom and still live to tell the story. The sword was at the missionary's throat when the executioner changed his mind and laid the cold steel down! Afterward the missionary was talking to a fellow missionary and said, "My first emotion was one of disappointment that he had not used the sword, because I thought I was being ushered into the presence of the King!" What insight!

In Durbanville's book, he made another striking observation, "To the believer, death comes, not like a policeman to drag the soul to an eternal prison house, but as a gentle hand that opens the door of the cage and lets the ransomed spirit fly to its native home in the skies," or beyond the blue!" The wise man Solomon knew of this event and described it this way, "Then shall the dust return to the earth as it was: and the spirit shall return unto God who gave it" (Ecclesiastes 12:7).

Just today Coleen, Marnie and I discussed Scott's funeral. We know we must take care of his body, but we are confident that God will take care of his spirit. And when Scott's soul departs, I will sing Fanny Crosby's famous lines from her song "My Saviour First of All":

> O the dear ones in Glory, how they beckon me to come,
> And our parting at the river I recall,
> To the sweet vale of Eden they will sing my welcome home,
> But I long to meet my Saviour first of all!

The second stanza I will sing comes from another favorite church hymn, "When My Life's Work is Ended":

> When my life's work is ended, and I cross the swelling tide.
> When the bright and glorious morning I shall see;
> I shall know my Redeemer when I reach the other side,
> And His smile will be the first to welcome me.

One of my favorite spiritual books is John Bunyan's world famous Pilgrim's Progress. One of the characters, Mr. Fearing, is a man who throughout all his life feared the crossing of The River of Death. Bunyan describes Mr. Fearing's arrival to the shores, *With water at a record low and not much above wetshod.* Mr. Fearing needed to know the words of the church hymn, "When I tread the verge of Jordan, bid my anxious fears subside!" The crossing into the shores of heaven must not be seen as a dreaded or dreary trip. Paul calls it a "gain," and "far better" (Philippians 2:21, 23). I read an article by a man who compiled some thoughts on this subject. He recorded these:

1. "Man is a sick fly, taking a dizzy ride on a gigantic wheel."

2. "Life is reasoning on the past, complaining of the present, and trembling for the future."

3. "Life is but a hollow bubble."

4. "The time man spends here has no more meaning than that of the humblest insect, crawling from one annihilation to another."

Is there any wonder why mankind is confused with hopelessness and helplessness that destroys the body, corrupts the soul, and decimates the spirit?

Compare and contrast how the Bible speaks of "beyond the blue" with what is written above. Heaven is a living place, for Jesus taught us that God was the God of the living not the dead (Matthew 22:32)! Heaven will be a delightful and a light-filled place (Revelation 21:23–25). Heaven will also be a love place (I John 4:7–12). Think of the loveliest day of your life; add the loveliest person of your life, and then compile all the loveliest memories of your life and combined they will not equal one second in the loveliest place God ever created! Compared to the death and dying of this plant, the gloom and doom on this earth, and the hatred and horrors of the world, who would not choose heaven? If I am wrong, I lose nothing, but if I am right, you will lose everything!

The primary problem why people do not believe in life "beyond the blue" is due to insight not sight. Sight has no value to a blind man (2 Corinthians 4:4) or a dead man (Ephesians 2:1). You can read spiritual books, listen to sermons and even read the Scriptures. But, unless you are given insight you will have no sight for higher ground. Johnson Oatman put it this way: "I want to scale the utmost height, and catch a gleam of glory bright." Only the Holy Spirit can take off the blinders and open the eyes to:

A land that is fair than day,
And by faith we can see it afar
For the Father waits over the way
To prepare us a dwelling place there.

We spend so much of our time seeing, "through a glass darkly" (1 Corinthians 13:12). We count the demons that hound, harass and haunt us in our last mile of the way. We forget to look up and see the angels surrounding us (Psalm 34:7). We have discovered that the valley of the shadow of death is filled with foes, doubts and dreads, insomnia and isolation, fears and tears and a myriad more. But, if we will raise our eyes to the canyon walls, we will discover as Elisha's servant did, "The mountain was full of horses and chariots of fire" (2 Kings 6:17). We must learn what Elisha taught, "They that be with us are more than they that be with them" (2 Kings 6:16). We look to the hope of life "beyond the blue!"

Chapter 33

Hard as Hemlock

DESPITE THE QUESTION MARK that hangs daily over our current situation, my spirit is encouraged by the exclamation point that has highlighted this trial so far. Today, I was reminded of what some call "The Lost Beatitude." The more famous beatitudes of Jesus are found in the opening sentences of His classic Sermon on the Mount (Matthew 5:1–12). Tucked away, however, in a conversation about John the Baptist, Jesus said, *"Blessed is he, whosoever shall not be offended in me"* (Matthew 11:6). I love the paraphrase of this verse that says, "Blessed is he who does not get upset by the way I run my business!" Throughout this test, I might have asked, "Why Scott? Why now?" I have never questioned God's right or business in this plan, however. My God is in charge, running on His own schedule and not mine. He is carrying out His plan for my son's life, and in the lives of my family as well. I believe this lost beatitude speaks directly as the question as to why John the Baptist was put in prison after his faithful service as the Messiah's forerunner. John would soon die, just like my son. There was no offense then and there is no offense now. My Savior does all things well!

John lived his dungeon days, just as my son is living his. Scott has not been out of his parsonage prison for over a month now. As John was likely shackled to the walls of his prison cell in Herod's fortress at Machaerus atop the Jordanian Plateau, so Scott is shackled to his recliner in the living room of our home. A prison can be made out of more than just rock, walls, iron bars and posted guards. A cage created by cancer, perhaps? Sentenced to death by beheading or sentenced to die by cancer? Is there a difference?

John sent some of his disciples to ask if Jesus was truly the Messiah, and in reply Jesus told the disciples to convey His miraculous works to John. Jesus then added, "I hope you won't be offended in me" I believe John the Baptist died believing that Jesus was the promised Messiah. John knew Jesus's ministry would increase as his ministry would decrease (John 3:30). I believe John was ready to die, and I believe, though Scott doesn't want to die, he is ready to die.

I am determined to get the blessing of the forgotten beatitude. I have decided to claim the happiness (blessing) that comes from not being offended of the Christ, or what Christ is doing to my family. I still do not understand why, but I am determined to not be offended despite the dungeon I endure with my son. I certainly have been frustrated, upset and even questioning. I will not, however, let cancer be a snare in my relationship with my Savior.

As I pondered this spiritual stubbornness to stay faithful and trust my Saviour through cancer, I remembered something I wrote on my fortieth birthday year. The words have helped me understand why cancer cannot cause me to be offended by what has happened to my son. I titled my thoughts, "Hard as Hemlock:"

"During a recent challenge to my youth group at Emmanuel Baptist Church, I encouraged them to pattern their lives after the hemlock tree. I chose this particular tree for its admirable attributes: flexible, firm and fruitful. I witnessed these traits in the homestead hemlocks of my boyhood and have cultivated them in my own life.

When I was a lad on my father's farm, I remember anytime we built or repaired something, we first went to the lumber pile for the boards needed. The Blackstone Homestead lumber yard was located behind the potato house in my Grandfather's apple orchard. You could find boards of every shape, size and selection. This private lumber yard had not been purchased from some retailer, but ever board had been created from a tree cut down from the Blackstone Homestead woods, as nearly half the homestead is forest. Every year when we would cut down dead or dying trees for burning, we set aside the best trees to be cut into lumber at Tupper's saw mill. Lumber was always available for the plank that needed replacing in the milking shed floor or rafter that had started to rot. My Dad, an avid tree lover, taught me the value of the hemlock tree and the planks it produced.

Why could the hemlock withstand the strain of such heavy loads? My father would say, "Look at them closely and notice their leaves are as delicate as fir, yet if you try to break a twig, you'll quickly learn the strength of its bough. It will bow and bend, but it will not break. It has been whipped by the winds for decades, but it has not yielded or been yanked apart. For the long months of a severe Maine winter, its graceful form may have been held down by a tremendous weight of snow, yet with the return of the warm spring sun its burden is lifted. The hemlock will straighten, proud and powerful. The hemlock is flexible." Dad would go on to tell how the root system stands undaunted, durable and ductile. He would remind me of the groves of huge hemlocks he had once discovered while hunting. The hemlock is a fruitful tree when it comes to producing other hemlocks.

When a strong, solid plank was needed, hemlock remained the only choice. Heavy, yes! Hard to handle, yes! Horrible to hammer, yes! But if you wanted something to bare a heavy load for a long period of time, a homestead hemlock was just the answer. Over forty years, I have felt that my roots in the homestead have given me the ability to bend and bow to the storms of life. However, it is only through the inner strength I have in the Lord Jesus Christ that I will never break, no matter the gale." (Philippians 4:13)

What was true then is also true now! I see in the lesson of the hemlock that one must be tough in order to fight an assault of cancer. Like the hemlock, you have to be flexible. Even amid the worst moments, the great Husbandman (John 15:1) looks for the fruit of obedience, not offense. He desires to see us remain true to Him through the prison. Is there any wonder why Jesus called John the Baptist the greatest born to a woman (Matthew 11:11)? I believe Jesus knew the heart of John, and He knew wilderness life had made John hard as a hemlock (Luke 1:80). A cancerous environment can break you or make you tougher. I have learned to bow to the winds of adversity, bend to the weight of burdens, and become stronger in the trials that come to make us better; so many have walked through the valley of cancer only to come out spiritually deformed on the other side. It is my desire, and by God's grace, that I survive these dungeon days unoffended by what the good Lord did to my son, his mother and me.

Chapter 34

More Like the Savior

TODAY IS TUESDAY. WE saw the homecare nurse for the twenty-first time. She came one week ago, and when she walked into the living room today, she cried. Scott has drastically changed. We love this nurse, not only because she has given Scott excellent care, but because she cares! Scott's countenance is thin and drawn. His eyes are yellow from jaundice. His arms and legs are bean poles. His feet are twice their normal size. His skin is thin, flesh over bone. His voice is shallow and confused. Scott's blood pressure is down and his breathing is increased. His oxygen levels are down, but his heart rate is up. He is not eating. His pain is magnified. I sit here pondering these medical changes in my son's condition. As I type, one question hits me like a ton of bricks. Does my son now look like my Savior did on the cross of Calvary?

Every historical article I have read about crucifixion, every image I have viewed, indicates that Jesus was just thin and drawn, as my son, if not more. The prophet David, in his psalm on the death of the Messiah, mentions, "I may tell all my bones: they look and stare upon me" (Psalm 22:17). You can see every bone, muscle and tendon on Scott's body. The veins in his neck and hands are like tiny tunnels, fully exposed on the surface of his skin. The Psalmist also wrote of Christ's crucifixion, "My strength is dried up like a potsherd; and my tongue cleaveth to my jaws; and thou hast brought me to the dust of death" (Psalm 22:15). I read this and realize it also depicts my son. He is having difficulty bringing his hand to his mouth or reaching up to scratch his brow. He cannot pull himself up to stand. Walking is beyond his capacity. His tongue is cleaving to the roof of his mouth. He is resisting death, but his mother and I, and the homecare nurse know death is near.

In all my years, I have never visited a dying man more than my son. I have seen withering away, but never to this extent. I have seen the emaciated, but not to the degree of Scott. I believe the Lord is giving me insight into just how frail my Savior's body was when He died on Golgotha's tree.

An unknown author once wrote:

> I asked a student what things he desired most." He said, "Books."
> I asked a miser, he cried, "Money."
> I asked a beggar, he faintly said, "Bread."
> I asked a drunkard, and he only called, "Alcohol!"
> I continued to ask those around me and I got answers like, "Wealth, fame, and pleasure."
> Finally I asked a poor man who had long displayed the character of an experienced Christian. He replied, "I greatly desire three things. First, that I may be found in Christ; second, that I may be like Christ; third, that I may be with Christ.

There is a story of the famous Christian missionary Adoniram Judson that highlights and underlines the precept of being more like the Savior. The story is told that Adoniram's wife once made the statement that she felt her husband was like one of the early apostles. When Judson heard the statement, he said, "I do not want to be like Paul, or any mere man. I want to be like Christ. I want to follow Him only, copy His teachings, drink in His Spirit, and place my feet in His footprints. Oh, to be more like Christ." We know we will never fully be like Christ until we see Him again (1 John 3:2–3). That doesn't mean we cannot come to understand Him better through insight like the cost of Jesus' death on the cross in relationship to His body.

I wish my son's condition on no man. My hope and desire is that I will never again watch someone die, as Scott is dying (Little did I know three years later almost to the day I watched Scott's mother go in a similar manner-look for it; I would also write a book of her departure called: "Why Not Me-A Diary of a Departure"!). In Scott's last lesson to me, he has granted me a different glimpse into how far my Savior was willing to go to gain my redemption. I sing the words of Fanny Crosby, "Thou my everlasting Portion, more than friend or life to me; all along my pilgrim journey, Saviour, let me walk with Thee." I know my son never dreamed that when he asked Jesus of Nazareth to be his Savior that he would end his life looking more like his Savior than his father. I sing the church hymn, "More Like Jesus:"

More about Jesus would I know,
More of His grace to others show;
More of His saving fullness see,
More of His love who died for me.

More about Jesus let me learn,
More of His holy will discern;
Spirit of God, my Teacher be,
Showing the things of Christ to me.

More about Jesus in His world,
Holding communion with my Lord,
Hearing His voice in every line,
Making each faithful saying mine.

More about Jesus on His throne,
Riches in glory all His own;
More of His kingdoms sure increase;
More of His coming, Prince of Peace.

More, more about Jesus;
More, more about Jesus;
More of His saving fulness see,
More of his love who died for me.

Sometimes we spend our whole lives doing other things and focused on other things. But as my son is learning in the end it is all about being "more about Jesus!"

Will I have to learn firsthand about this aspect of the death of Christ? Will the experience I am now sharing with my son be enough? The Lord knows the answer to this question. Despite this bitter trial and these agonizing days watching my son go to his Calvary, I am determined more than ever to keep singing Charles H. Gabriel's song (More like the Master) as my prayer:

More like the Master I would ever be,
More of His meekness, more humility
More zeal to labor, more courage to be true,
More consecration for work He bids me do

More like the master is my daily prayer;
More strength to carry crosses I must bear
More earnest effort to bring His kingdom in;
More of His Spirit, the wanderer to win

More like the Master I would live and grow;
More of His love to others I will show,
More self-denial, like His in Galilee;
More like the Master I long to ever be.

Take thou my heart; I would be thine alone
Take thou my heart and make it all thine own.
Purge me from sin, O Lord, I now implore.
Wash me and keep me, thine forever more.

I learned long ago that I am an audio-visual-hands-on learner. I am a 1 John 1:1 learner, "That which was from the beginning (II Timothy 3:15), which we have heard, which we have seen with our eyes, which we have looked upon, and our hands have handled, of the Word of life." I have sat in many classrooms over my lifetime. I have listened to many a teacher. I have read book after book. My best training, however, has come through experiences like I am having with Scott, up close and personal, hands-on and in my face. For the last one hundred and eighty days, I have been in the classroom of suffering, taught by my teacher, Scott Alexander Blackstone. Today, he taught me about my Savior's body on the cross.

Chapter 35

The Blue Book

BEFORE SCOTT'S DIAGNOSIS WITH neuroendocrine carcinoma, the only "blue book" I had ever known was "The Kelly Blue Book," a listing for what old cars might be worth. Considering the current world of computers, Google and iPhones, most people might not even remember the old Kelly Blue Book. How many would recognize the "end of life" book, called by professionals the "blue book?"

The title on the front of this blue book reads, Gone from My Sight: The Dying Experience, by Barbara Karnes, RN. The term "blue book" simply comes from the color of the booklet, just thirteen pages long. Karnes writes on the first page:

"Each person approaches death in their own way, bringing to this last experience their own uniqueness. What is listed here is simply a guideline, a road map. Like any map, there are many roads arriving at the same destination, and many ways to enter the same city. Use this guideline while remembering there is nothing concrete here; all is very, very flexible. Any one of the signs in this booklet may be present; all may be present; none may be present. For some, it will take months to separate from the physical body, for others, only minutes. Death comes in its own time, in its own way. Death is as unique as the individual who is experiencing it."

I will begin by saying that Karnes blue book is a nurse's look at death, a very humanistic view of death. There is another Good Book that also takes a good look at death and dying, and unlike Karnes does not give control to death. Karnes' book suggests that death is in control, while the Good

Book is clear, "I am He (Jesus) that liveth, and was dead; and, behold, I am alive for evermore, Amen; and have the keys to hell and death" (Revelation 1:18). I agree with Karnes' observation to a degree, especially considering her pedigree as an International Humanitarian Woman of the Year (2015) recipient. She has witnessed the passing of people a plethora of times, and her insights have helped multitudes. But, if one chooses to not see death from the other side, that individual is not getting a full picture of what it means to die or how to die well!

Last year, my brother Michael went through a similar experience as we are with his god-daughter, a young woman in her late twenties who died within a year of being diagnosed with a terminal brain tumor. After Michael heard through family that we were in the final days with Scott's cancer, he texted me last night and shared that in his god-daughter's final days, they talked more of the things of heaven, than the things of earth. Within this book, I too have on occasion focused beyond the physical dying, but rather focused on the land where Scott is going. Interestingly, Karnes makes mention of this possibility at the end of her book when she says:

"How we approach death is going to depend upon our fear of life, how much we participated in that life, and how willing we are to let go of this known expression to venture into a new one. Fear and unfinished business are two big factors in determining how much resistance we put into meeting death. The separation becomes complete when breathing stops. What appears to be the last breath is often followed by one or two long spaced breaths and then the physical body is empty. The owner is no longer in need of a heavy, nonfunctioning vehicle. They have entered a new city, a new life.

"Before I speak of the city I hope Karnes refers to, let us make it very clear from Scripture what death is really like. The medical profession has one definition, but the Bible says this, "Then shall the dust return to the earth as it was: and the spirit shall return unto God who gave it" (Ecclesiastes 12:7).

Let me share with you from the greatest Book ever written, what I hope Karnes is referring to as the "new city, new life." I will begin with the words of the great nineteenth century preacher Charles Spurgeon:

"The city is of heavenly and divine birth, shaped and built by God in heavenly mold with heavenly air about her. The heavenly life will come from God directly, and will be heavenly, not earthly. Many earthly things, by chance, by happenings and of direct purpose and appointment, shaped our earthly lives, but in a direct and more evident and all inclusive way, our heavenly lives will be from God, and the air and conditions of heaven will shape the. Earth will be forgotten, but the former things will scarcely be remembered. Nor will the things of old be considered, but crowded out, overwhelmed and retired by the magnificent grandeur, ever new and expanding glories of the present. Earth will be too little; it's most sacred relations, its most pleasing things all too poor to come into mind in heaven."

Yes, there is a city just like Atlanta, New York, Dallas, and a myriad of others here on this earth. Just as the earthly cities are real, so is the heavenly one that long, long ago even Abraham sought, *"For he looked for a city which hath foundations, whose builder and maker is God"* (Hebrews 11:10). This city has been the focus of many for a millennium. Our Book tells us these truths about our new city and new life:

1. Heaven is a city of life because the Living God abides there (Revelation 21:1; John 1:4). Life is the Glory of God and all that come to this place will have everlasting life (Revelation 7:9–12; 22:1–2).

2. Heaven is a city of light because the "Light of the World" (Revelation 21:11, 23–24; John 9:5) abides there. Death is often pictured on earth as darkness or blackness (the Black Plague comes to mind), but the departure of the saints will be as many have experiences it and come back to tell us like walking towards a bright light! (I John 2:8)

3. Heaven is a city of love because "God is love," and where God is there is love (I John 4:8; I Peter 2:7). The world speaks of love, searches for love, but even in the city of brotherly love there is little love. Heaven will be a totally different experience in the area of love, a charity that will never be separated.

4. Heaven is a city of lines because it is being built on the pattern of foursquare, a 1500 mile cube, where the architect of the universe has drawn up the plans, dug the foundations, and laid out the gates (Revelation 21:16; 21:19–20; 21:21; 21:17).

5. Heaven is the city of the Lamb because Jesus will also be there (Revelation 21:22; John 1:29). There will be no need of a temple, a church, cathedral, or any chapels because Jesus will be there.

6. Heaven is a city of loveliness because of the unparalleled beauty of the rare building materials of gold, jasper and pearl (Revelation 21:18 ; I Corinthians 2:9). Compared to the best man can offer here, only the most precious, richest, rarest, and most lovely will be there.

7. Heaven is a city of longevity because the New Jerusalem will be made to last, unlike the cities of the world today (Revelation 22:3–5; 21:10). It is an "eternal city" for an eternal God and an eternal people (Romans 6:23).

Oh that Hospice would pass out the Good Book alongside the "the blue book," so people getting ready to depart can have all the facts.

Chapter 36

Cancer is so Limited

ONE OF THE FIRST letters of encouragement my son received upon his diagnosis was the following anonymous prose entitled, "Cancer Is So Limited:"

It cannot cripple LOVE
It cannot shatter HOPE
It cannot corrode FAITH
It cannot destroy CONFIDENCE
It cannot kill FRIENDSHIP
It cannot shut out MEMORIES
It cannot silence COURAGE
It cannot invade the SOUL
It cannot destroy PEACE
It cannot quench the SPIRIT
It cannot lessen the POWER OF THE RESURRECTION
It cannot steal ETERNAL LIFE

Our greatest enemy is not disease, but despair. Keep trusting God's love so your spirit will remain strong. If the cancer has invaded your life, refuse to let it touch your spirit. Your body can be severely afflicted and you have great struggle, but if you trust in God's love, your spirit will remain strong.

As I reread these words this morning, the 180th day of this journey, I was reminded of a few other experiences that cancer has been limited to touch. I add my own additions to the prose:

It has not divided our FAMILY
It has not broken our RESOLVE
It has not changed our MINDS
It has not affected the CHURCH
It has not distracted our ATTENTION
It has not detoured our FOCUS
It has not discouraged our TRUST
It has not diminished our CARE
It has not deflected our FAITHFULNESS
It has not altered our GOAL
It has not weakened our PURPOSE
It has not swiped out our DREAMS
It has not lessened our CHARITY
It has not taken away our JOY
It has not multiplied our SORROWS
It has not added to our BURDENS
It has not driven away our SUPPORTERS
It has not blotted out our GOD

I imagine before this trial is over I will add to this list. My son has taken the blows of this disease, and has stayed strong in his faith that cancer will not journey with him to heaven. So, as Scott stands on "Jordan's stormy banks, and cast a wishful eye to Canaan's fair and happy land," he is like the ship that Henry Van Dyke mentions in his classic line:

"I am standing upon the seashore. A ship at my side spreads her white sails to the morning breeze and starts for the blue ocean. She is an object of beauty and strength. I stand and watch her until at length she hangs like a speck of white cloud just where the sea and sky come to mingle with each other. Then someone at my side says, 'There, she is gone!' Gone where? Gone from my sight. That is all. She is just as large in mast and hull and spar as she was when she left my side and she is just as able to bear the load of living freight to her destined port. Her diminished size is in me, not in her. And just as the moment when someone at my side says, 'There, she is gone!' There are other eyes watching her coming, and other voices ready to take up the glad shout, 'Here she comes!' And that is dying."

Others liken death and the journey to heaven like a railway ride, "Life is like a mountain railway, with an engineer that's brave." Make it a sailing ship, train, plane, car or the like; there is one aspect we must all agree upon: there will be no cancer on your ship, plane or train.

Many years ago I put together a sermon about heaven focusing on the "no more" list in Revelation 2: no more sea (1), death (4), temple (22), sun (23), entrance (27). I have added a few of my own things to this list that I believe will not be in heaven. There will be no more water filters or bottled water, as the water of heaven is pure (Revelation 22:1). There will be no more light switches or light bills (Revelation 22:5). There will be no more locked doors or crime (Revelation 21:27). Nothing will need to be repaired (Revelation 21:5). This is an excellent prospect for me, a useless handyman here on earth. There will be no more accidents or injuries (Revelation 21:4). There will be no more neighbor troubles (Revelation 7:9, 21:3). Who will your neighbor be, I wonder? There will be no more refrigerators and freezers, as our food will be fresh off the tree (Revelation 22:2). There will be no more cancer or sickness (Revelation 21:4). Scott will enter heaven cancer free. His home-going will be absent from any sickness or disease.

I love the story about a missionary who was disembarking from a ship after a long voyage from a lifetime mission field. As he came off the gangplank, he saw a very large crowd of people gathered at the end and more on the dock. The mass of people were waving banners and shouting, "Welcome Home!" As it happened, he was on the same passenger ship from Africa with Theodore Roosevelt, who was returning from a big-game hunting expedition. As the crowd engulfed the famous man and carried him away, there was left on the dock a single individual, a friend of the missionary, and the only greeter for recognition of the decades of service for the Lord in a dark and dangerous place. As they walked away together, the friend commented the missionary, "It is you who deserves this welcome, rather than Teddy!" The humble missionary replied, "Don't be concerned, I'm not home yet!" No matter the affliction, no matter the alignment, none can affect your home-coming!

Chapter 37

Where the Roses Never Fade

WE JUST FINISHED OUR fifth meeting with Kate, one of our Hospice nurses. Her visit is two days early due to Scott's worsening condition. Danielle came yesterday and requested Kate come today for an additional evaluation. Kate feels Scott will live mere days. Scott fell again this morning and his breathing is getting more difficult. It is impossible for him to stand on his own. I picked up the mail on the way home and found two more letters of encouragement and support. People around the world have responded to Scott's trial and our test with loving prayer and cards. It seems that no matter where I go these days someone focuses their attention toward our care. Just last Sunday, the worship team chose their songs in hopes of encouraging us. One song in particular touched my heart. Here are the words to "Where the Roses Never Fade":

> I am going to a city where the streets are golden laid,
> Where the Tree of Life is blooming and the roses never fade.
> In this world we have our troubles. Satan's snares we must evade.
> We'll be free from all temptation where the roses never fade.
>
> Loved one's gonna to be with Jesus in the place of endless day.
> They are waiting for my coming where the roses never fade.
>
> Here they bloom for but a season, soon their beauty is decayed.
> I am going to a city, where the roses never fade.

They finished their song set with the words from "Going Home":

Passing from that lonesome valley
We will meet our loved ones there,
And we shall see our home in glory
When we climb that golden stairs.

When we finally win the victory
And our work on earth is done,
Then we shall see our Blessed Saviour;
Wing our praise for God's dear Son.

We're going home, to be with Jesus,
Going home, some sweet day.
Where we shall see our Blessed Saviour,
Who has saved us and shown us the way!

While home for lunch, I administered Scott's medications. I helped him go to the bathroom for the hundredth time or more. I picked him off the floor for the fifth time. I put his oxygen mask back on and settled him in his recliner, covering him with his fleece. In many ways, this half year has drug along, yet in other respects it has rapidly flown. The baby monitor by Scott's chair only picks up faint cries. Despite the advance of technology, Scott fell only because his faint cry for help was so weak. I sat at my desk compiling this book believing both Scott and Coleen were sleeping safe and sound. I was wrong, but no more! Our hopes of a miracle have passed. God has made that clear. Our prayers for a full recovery have gone the way of our hope. My hopeful message of a dramatic and miraculous "I told you so! God worked!" will not be uttered. Rather, I change my message to, "God makes no mistakes and all He does is right." There is no stereotype way in which God works. He delivered Peter from prison, but left John the Baptist in a dungeon to die. I accept whatever God does, however He does it. Why do I have such belief? Because no matter what lies ahead for Scott's end, we believe he will go to "where the roses never fade!"

As we talked to Kate this afternoon, we showed her our son in his prime, a uniformed soldier in the United States ARMY. We told her stories of his birth and his early days as a jaundiced baby. What irony he will die a jaundices thirty-nine year old. I told her how I had assisted a midwife deliver Scott on November 7, 1977. I shared I was determined to be with him on his last day on earth, as I was with him on his first. We spoke of our faith, an old-time faith that has allowed us to not surrender or shirring in the face of our foe called cancer. I will not moan and mourn his falling breaths, weakened form or yellowing flesh. Whatever life remains for Scott, his mother and I will live it with him. This is the promise we made as new parents on the day of his birth, and the promise we made in October as old parents. Our jaw is set. Our hands are clenched to hold on and hang on until the end, even if it is amid tear dimmed eyes. Why do we do this? Because we believe Scott is going to a place "where the roses never fade."

My comfort comes in knowing that whatever my son, my wife, my daughter and I are facing, our Savior has already endured. He is leading us through this valley. Our Lord could weep at the side of his friend Lazarus' tomb, but also set His face towards home (John 11; 14:1–2). We are now living the earthly emotions mixed with heavenly hope. Coleen told me today that after I went to bed last night she and Scott had a good heart-to-heart. In that conversation, she told him it was alright for him to go; he did not have to fight any longer on our account; we would be fine; his death would make us so sad, and yet so happy. I have come to believe this final statement is all about spiritual proportion: balance. A great overlooked Biblical precept is, "Let your moderation be known to all men" (Philippians 4:5). Spiritual balance (moderation) is important at times like this. We must guard against being so overcome with grief that we fail to appreciate the grace of God. We can be happy and horrified at the same time, if proper moderation is applied to the situation or circumstance. Happy to think of our son in gloryland cancer free, pain free and at peace, yet horrified to think of the moments here on earth before he sees the roses that never fade!

I have come to believe we do not have to choose one emotion. We can be stoic as we approach our son's death and sentimental to his departure. There is balance that our Savior exhibited to which we can pattern our response. My wife and I are trying to showcase this moderation before the unbelievers who have helped us through this valley. We have been surrounded by a myriad of saints throughout this challenge that understand our actions. We are concerned, however, for those who question why we believe the way we do and are acting as we are. I know we are always in a dangerous situation when we bring an unbeliever into our circle of supporters, especially in a situation like cancer in a man as young as my son. We will be forced to answer difficult questions. While I might not be able to have all the answers, I can show them I am fully confident in my belief of the Lord's goodness amid the valley, and my hope in the place beyond the bend and beyond the blue where the roses never fade.

Chapter 38

Beyond the Borderland

I BELIEVE THIS OLD world is "heaven's borderland," and I believe my son is treading toward that borderland as I write. I am now writing these chapters from the dining room of our home. I started the "departure" vigil for my son at midnight last night. Hospice feels we have moved from days to hours. The transition to this reality happened quickly, as just a few days ago we believed he had weeks to live. Tomorrow will be exactly six months since this journey began, and today I am unsure if he'll make it to tomorrow.

So many that crosses into "heaven's borderland" rally for a few minutes, hours or even days. It appears this will not be our story. My wife had the final talk with Scott last night, just before midnight when I took over so she could sleep. Sleep has evaded her for almost twenty-four hours. So, it was crucial for her to get some rest before the end. She sang to him of heaven. Amid her singing, Scott told her he had seen into heaven. She once again told him he could go and not to worry about us. I think Scott knew nearly eighteen hours ago that he had crossed into "heaven's borderland." He is ready to give up the good fight and yield to the embrace of his Savior. Scott is leaving us for a better land. But, as an anonymous poet once wrote, "Death can hide but not divide; thou art but on Christ's other side; thou are with Christ with Christ with me, united in Christ are we."

There is a lot of singing in "heaven's borderland," and not much talking. The songs of the saints provide great comfort for not only the loved ones, but the patient entering "heaven's borderland." My wife has taken our church hymnal and flips through its pages, sings the songs she loves while holding Scott's hand. Many believe the last thing to go is a person's hearing. I believe this to be true. So, as our son walks through "heaven's borderland," he is listening to the sweet tones of his mother's voice, singing the songs of the saints. Jeremy Taylor has written, "Happy will I be and forever happy, if after death I might hear the melody of those hymns and hallelujahs which the citizens of that celestial kingdom and the squadron of those blessed spirits sing in praise of the eternal King."

I believe the melodic sounds of my wife will soon be silenced by the celestial choirs, as Scott arrives beyond the borderland, somewhere beyond the blue. My mind drifts to beyond the borderland, to that *"fair and happy land where my possessions lie."* 1 Peter 1:4 speaks of an "incorruptible inheritance" that awaits us. Another anonymous author gives this insight:

"My race is run; my warfare over; the solemn hour is nigh, when offered up to God, my soul shall wing its flight on high. With heavenly weapons I have fought the battles of the Lord, finished my course and kept the faith, depending on His Word. Henceforth there is laid up for me a crown which cannot fade; the righteous Judge at that great day shall place it on my head. Nor hath the Sovereign Lord decreed this prize for me alone, but for all such as love like me the appearing of His Son. From every snare and evil work His grace shall me defend, and to His heavenly Kingdom safe shall bring me in the end!"

I have come to these conclusions about this inheritance of which the author speaks. First, our incorruptible inheritance is a reward for faithful service here on earth (Colossians 3:24). I love the saying, *"Spiritual investments always bear heavenly interest."* Second, our incorruptible inheritance is because of a relationship (Romans 8:15–17; Galatians 4:6–7). The relationship has less to do with us and more about Him, as we share in Christ's inheritance as joint-heirs and brothers (John 1:12). Third, our incorruptible inheritance is reserved (1 Peter 1:4). Our inheritance has been reserved beyond the borderland in heaven. Often times, preachers ask, "Have you made your reservation for heaven?" The theology behind this question is simple and based on Christ's promise to prepare a place for us (John 1:1–4). In order to take advantage of our place, we must have our names written down in the logbook (Revelation 21:27).

The heavenly reserves are imperishable, unfading and untouchable (Matthew 6:19–21). All that heaven has in store awaits its heirs beyond the borderland. What a glorious inheritance is waiting there! What a pleasing and promising prospect! A man by the name of Philip Doddridge reflects on this saying, "Blest Saviour, introduced by Thee, have I my race begun; and, crowned with victory, at Thy foot I'll lay my honors down. This God's all-animating voice that calls thee from on high; this His own hand presents the prize to thine aspiring eye; that prize, with peerless glories bright, which shall new luster boast, when victors' wreaths and monarchs' gems shall blend in common dust." What wondrous wealth awaits Scott and those who follow him through heaven's borderland.

Years ago, I read of a woman who crossed the Atlantic Ocean to visit her daughter, Martha. A terrible storm engulfed the ship, threatening to sink the vessel and drown all the passengers. The captain, in an attempt to calm the passengers, went from cabin to cabin giving words of instructions should the worst come to be. He eventually came to the cabin of this elderly saint and rather than hearing panic, he heard singing. He assumed she must be mad with fear and said, "Madam, do you know our ship my sink at any moment? How can you sing at a time like this?" The dear woman replied, "I have two daughters, Martha who lives in New York City and Mary, who has lived in Heaven fifteen years. If the ship does not sink, I'll be with Martha in the morning. If the ship sinks, I'll be with Mary in glory. Either way, it will be a happy meeting!" What a beautiful attitude! Oh that we would have the same confidence in our last hour!

I have shared these thoughts before, but thought them worth repeating in the context of what awaits our son beyond the borderland. An anonymous author wrote, "Passing out of the shadow, into the purer light; stepping behind the curtain, getting a clearer sight; passing out of the darkness into eternal day; why do we call it dying, this sweet going away?" The great beyond remains a mystery on many levels, but I am grateful for the glimpses of glory the Bible allows me to see.

Chapter 39

"I See Jesus"

THE CROSSOVER MOMENT BEGAN on Wednesday night for my son. I had gone to bed early in the evening knowing in a few short hours I would take up my nightly vigil in the recliner next to Scott. My wife and I knew the days were with him were drawing to a close. Unbeknownst to me, my wife determined that Wednesday would be the night she would let her son go to glory. As Coleen sat next to him, she told him once again it was okay to go and we would be alright. She assured him he had fought the good fight, but the struggle was too much, he needed to let God take him. Coleen decided to sing a few hymns with him. Having turned off the lights, she sang the precious truths of our faith from memory. When the grief and reality of this valley of the shadow of death overcame her, she hummed her way through the conclusion of a hymn. When this singspiration finished, Scott opened his eyes wide and said, *"I see Jesus!"* Excited by his statement, Coleen asked, "What do you see, son?" He described a beautiful white brightness, and fell back asleep. Scott would be in heaven three days later, never awaking from a drug induced coma.

I have often wondered if this simple phrase, "I see Jesus!" might have been on the lips of those who saw Jesus after His resurrection. Is that what Mary Magdalene said when she returned from the garden tomb (John 20:18)? Is that what the two disciples on the road to Emmaus said when they returned to Jerusalem to announce their meeting and supper with the Lord (Luke 24:33)? Is that what Peter, James, Paul and the other disciples said after their encounter with Jesus and what of the five hundred (I Corinthians 15:5–8)?

As I pondered my wife's last encounter with her beloved son, I recalled two songs with my son's last words, "I see Jesus!" The first song tells of a post ascension sighting by the Churches first deacon, Stephen, who would eventually be stoned for his faith in Christ. The Apostle Luke records, "But he (Stephen), being full of the Holy Ghost, looked up steadfastly into heaven, and saw the glory of God and Jesus standing on the right hand of God. And said, Behold, I see the heavens opened, and the Son of man standing on the right hand of God" (Acts 7:55–56). Songwriter Hank Snow wrote "I See Jesus":

> Once a man named Stephen preached about the Lord;
> Folks were saved then folks were healed as they heard his word.
> Satan did not like it and soon he had his crowd,
> And as he was tried that day, Stephen cried aloud.
> I see Jesus standing at the Father's right hand.
> I see Jesus over in the Promised Land.
> Work is over now, I'm coming to Thee.
> I see Jesus standing waiting for me.
>
> As the stones fell on him beating out his life;
> Stephen knew he'd soon be through with all toil and strife.
> So much like the Master with a heart so true;
> He prayed, "Lord, forgive them for they know not what they do!"
> I see Jesus standing at the Father's right hand.
> I see Jesus over in the Promised Land.
> Work is over now, I'm coming to Thee.
> I see Jesus standing waiting for me.
>
> Through the gate of glory and down streets of gold,
> Marched the hero of the Lord into heaven's fold.
> When he met the Saviour at the great white throne;
> I believe He smiled and said, "Stephen, welcome home."
> I see Jesus standing at the Father's right hand.
> I see Jesus over in the Promised Land.
> Work is over now, I'm coming to Thee.
> I see Jesus standing waiting for me

The great evangelist George Whitefield once said, *"You take care of your life, let the Lord takes care of your death!"* This is what my wife and I did after Scott's final three words. We placed our son once more in the hands of our Savior. Then I recalled the fine words from the country singer Cristy Lane who sings, "I See Jesus in Every Tear I Cry":

I didn't see the teardrops fall in the garden when He cried.
I didn't see the nail scarred hands or where they pierced His side.
I don't know what Jesus saw as He looked through tear-filled eyes,
But I see Jesus in every tear I cry.

I didn't see the crown of thorns they placed upon His head.
I didn't see the strips He bore or hear the words He said.
I didn't see the blood that flowed from Calvary when he died,
But I see Jesus in every tear I cry.

I didn't see the empty tomb where my Saviour laid.
I didn't see the stone rolled away, but I know that He lives today.
I don't know when He's coming back to take His waiting bride,
But I see Jesus in every tear I cry!

I see Jesus, in every tear that falls.
I feel His presence now; He hears me when I call.
I don't know what others see when they look through tear-filled eyes,
But I see Jesus in every tear I cry.

These are the words express what Coleen and I felt during the last three days of our son's earthly existence. My prayer is that you have not heard one note of defeat in these chapters, no hint of tragedy in these articles, and no suggestion of regret in this book. I pray you haven't heard a throbbing dirge or death march, but the triumphal and glorifying words of the "Hallelujah Chorus." Who among us would not want to see Jesus and look in his face? I believe the Good Lord gives His children a peek into what lies before them just before their departure date. What joy to a mother's heart and a father's soul to think that our son no longer sees temporal faces, but eternal ones, and better yet, the face of Christ Himself (2 Corinthians 4:18)!

Chapter 40

Crossing Over

IN THE TIME IT took me to walk from our living room to the kitchen, Scott was gone. I had rested beside his recliner from Thursday morning until Saturday morning. My wife supplemented the vigil I kept, alternating days and nights. We wanted to be next to him until the end, just as we were in the beginning. His crossing over was so peaceful and quiet, however, it took me a few minutes to recognize he had stopped breathing. Many say that regardless of the time of passing, whether expected or unexpected, there is inevitable shock, grim blow and sad end. For me, however, this was not the case. My feeling at 6:16 a.m. on April 1, 2017, was simply that Scott was gone. My boy had crossed over. The lad I called son departed for a better place, and I could not nor would not wish him back. When I went upstairs to tell his mom, I found the same calmness, the same tearless eyes. I found the same acceptance that Scott was simply gone. His cancer ridden body remained, but Scott, our precious boy had crossed over.

Scott's departure meant the loss of many routine events in our lives. As we changed his clothes and cleaned him up for Jordan's Funeral home to pick up his body, Co and I talked about these things. Gone would be the daily phone calls from Scott on his way home from work. Coleen so looked forward to those daily conversations with her son. Gone were the visits home to take a few days to fish the local ponds and streams of his youth. Gone were the texts to tell us daily happenings. Gone was his spirit of joy, despite all he endured, he never complained!! Gone are the golf clubs, fishing poles, and Harley Davidson paraphernalia. While Scott might be gone from us physically, there are a few things that remain.

His God remains. We are so thankful for this truth amid our supreme bereavement. I can honestly say this has been the most difficult home going of them all (Little did I know that a more difficult separation was in my future when like Scott I would be at the bedside of Scott's mother when just three short years later she would die of liver failure-I also wrote a book about that sad goodbye under the title of "Why Not Me-a diary of a departure!), despite losing my Grandfather Blackstone in 1975, or my father-in-law in 1997, my best friend and cousin Bob in 2012, or my father just a few months before! Nothing before this can measure up to this homegoing. I have to keep remembering is that Scott is gone, and I am going too, someday. Someday the picture will change, and we will use that word again.

The book of Revelation tells us of the glorious theology of "gone." What about all those tears? Gone! What about death itself? Gone! What about the sorrows and sickness? Gone! What about pain? Gone! What about separation? Gone! What about cancer? Gone! What about sin? Gone! (Revelation 21:4) I was reminded today of Vance Havner and his words when his wife Sara crossed over:

> "Dear one, you are not gone, just gone on ahead.
> And I would say, in lines precious to me:
> Should you go first and I remain, one thing I'd have you do:
> Walk slowly down the path of death, for soon I'll follow you!
> I'll want to know each step you take,
> I'll want to walk the same,
> For some day down that lonely road,
> You'll hear me call your name!"

The famous eighteenth century commentator Matthew Henry offers comfort for the "going":

> "Would you like to know where I am? I am at home in my Father's house, in the mansions prepared for me here. I am where I want to be-no longer on the stormy sea, but in God's safe, quiet harbor. My sowing time is done and I am reaping; my joy is as the joy of harvest. Would you like to know how it is with me? I am made perfect in holiness. Grace is swallowing up in glory. Would you like to know what I am doing? I see God, not through a glass darkly, but face to face. I am engaged in the sweet enjoyment of my precious Redeemer. I am singing hallelujahs to Him who sits upon the throne, and I am constantly praising Him. Would you know what blessed company I keep? It is better than the best of earth. Here are the holy angels and the spirits of just men made perfect. . ..I am with many of

my old acquaintance with whom I worked and prayed, and who have come here before me. Lastly, would you know how long this will continue? It is the dawn that never fades! After millions and millions of ages, it will be as fresh as it is now. Therefore, weep not for me!"

I know the human eye is incapable, and the human ear is unable and the human heart has no capacity to understand or imagine what happened when my son went beyond the blue (I Corinthians 2:9). I am confident, however, that I know where he has gone. I am assured by the Bible that he is safe and well in God's abode! I love these words by M. R. DeHaan of the "Our Daily Bread" staff who wrote:

"The moment I leave on a trip, I immediately begin thinking of the time when I'll be coming back again. Home-comings are usually happy occasions. We look forward to visiting our childhood scenes, meeting our old friends, and reliving in our imaginations the experiences of youth. The believer also looks forward to that grand "home-coming" reserved for the saints of God. The Christian is a stranger in this world and a pilgrim (I Peter 2:11). His citizenship is in Heaven (Philippians 3:20). Who can visualize that scene when our Lord shouts from the air, and all the dead in Christ are raised? Then the living believers, changed in a moment, will be caught up together with them to meet the Lord in the air! This 'home-coming' will be a double meeting. First we shall meet our saved loved ones, and then, united with them, we shall rise to meet the Lord in the air. Note: we shall greet our saved loved ones first. Then we shall be caught up together-to meet the Lord (I Thessalonians 4:17). That will be the grand climax of the "home-coming" to be received and be greeted by our Lord Himself."

I can hardly fathom that my son has already experienced this greeting, having met both the Lord and his loved ones that have travelled on before him. I will close this chapter with these words I have had tucked away for many years by an unknown author:

"The endless theme, earth and heaven will pass away; it's not a dream God will make all things new that day. Gone is the curse from which I stumbled and fell; evil is banished to eternal hell. See now the nations bow down to sing; it's only sound is the praises to Christ, the King. Slowly the names from the books are read, I know the King, and there is no need to dread. See over there, it's a mansion prepared for me; where I can live with my Saviour eternally. No more night, no more pain, no more tears, never crying again. Praise to the great "I am;" we will live in the light of the risen Lamb!"

I experienced zero doubt on Scott's last earthly day: months and days and hours and minutes that God could have still delivered him from death. Whether He could or would be in the hands of the Almighty. We now know His divine will. Scott was to go, depart, crossover!

Postlude

Beyond the Bend

THIS TRIBUTE TO SCOTT's battle with lung and liver cancer has included my thoughts about "beyond the blue" and "beyond the borderland." I must write of one more "beyond" before concluding this work, and why I called this book by this title. Exactly twenty years ago, our family fought a similar battle with my father-in-law, Stacy Meister. Despite the similarities, the biggest difference between Scott and his grandfather comes down to time. Stacy lasted four hundred and thirty-five days, while Scott lasted only one hundred and eighty-three. Stacy spent nearly a solid year hunting and fishing and enjoying all life has to offer. Scott enjoyed not a single round of golf or motorcycle ride. He did manage one hour of bass fishing with me, his Dad, at Toddy Pond when he first arrived in Maine. Stacy got out and about, while Scott's weakness confined him to the parsonage. Stacy felt pretty good up until the last few months, while Scott remained in misery from the beginning. There is one more similarity that struck me as I prepared this book. The title "Beyond the Bend," actually comes from the journal (A Diary of a Departure) I kept during Stacy's departure. Periodically throughout Stacy's trial, I would write my thoughts on a significant event or particular day of struggle. This is what I wrote on August 19, 1996:

Stacy's funeral service began to take shape in my thoughts today. He has asked me to deliver the message at his funeral, a difficult task to be sure. I felt it important to gather a few thoughts before his actual departure, lest I lack clarity of thought. I found the title for the service from an Our Daily

Bread devotional that inspired me. Frank Boreham (1871–1959) wrote "Wisps of Wildfire:"

"A few weeks ago, in a small boat, I was making my way up one of the most picturesque of our Australian (this jumped off the page to me because I had spent 68-days in Western Australia in the summer of 1972) rivers. The forestry on both banks was magnificent beyond description. . .A canoe gilded ahead of us. Presently, the waters seem to come to an end. . .. We watched the canoe, and to our astonishment, it simply vanished! When we came to the point at which the canoe had so mysteriously disappeared, we beheld a sudden twist in the river artfully concealed by the tangle of bush. The blind alley was no blind alley at all."

Then, making a reference to the believer when he departs this world for another Boreham wrote:

"They have gone on like the canoe. It had turned a bend in the river; they have turned a bend in the road of life!" As I ponder how I wanted to share when my fishing partner departs this earth, I will say that he is merely "beyond the bend." Soon we will catch up and round the corners together again we will be. I also found this in an old Our Daily Bread article:

"Some years ago a dear friend of mine suddenly "took the wings of the morning" and departed to be with Jesus. Recalling his witness and his favorite hymn, I penned a bit of verse that was read at his funeral. Today, the Lord brought that almost forgotten poem back to mind, and I feel I must pass it on to you that it may comfort some pilgrim of sorrow passing through 'the valley of Baca' (Psalm 84:6) who this very day needs the assurance that the Lord is eternally catching all our tears in "the bottle" (Psalm 56:8) of His remembrance. Bearing in mind my belief in ". . .absent from the body. . ." means ". . .present with the Lord. . ." (2 Corinthians 5:8). I wrote this: Only passed beyond the shadows to that land of endless day, only held in sweet communion where the tears have passed away. You are blending with the angels in their chorus "round the Throne," now you'll never more sorrow, you've a mansion all your own! You have met the lovely Bridegroom, and the friends who've gone before, and you would not journey earthward, though you love us as of yore; for your hands are filled with treasures, and your soul is thrilled with grace, joy we cannot half imagine, now reflects from your dear face. Oh, so suddenly you left us for your mansion in the sky; in the twinkling you were raptured, you could scarcely say "goodbye!" But we'll meet you soon in Heaven, when our pilgrimage shall end, and we'll say a glad "Good morning" where we'll never part again! While on earth you loved to hear it, a sweet hymn we now recall, "Though I cannot understand it, yet I know, He knows it all." This a comfort as we sorrow, and the "thorns our way opposes," that in Heaven grows the roses, all the rest my

Father knows! We shall journey on with patience, brave in Jesus' precious name, till the day we meet in Heaven, oh, so changed, but still the same. And your memory will be blessed, as this earth we sadly roam, and we'll live the more for Jesus, who has brought you safely Home!"

I believed all these things about Stacy's homegoing, and twenty years later I still believe it all about Scott's homegoing. Scott and Stacy are "beyond the bend," as they were on that fishing trip when three generations came together to fish. The grandfathers (Wendell Blackstone and Stacy Meister), the fathers (Barry Blackstone and Larry Fox, my brother-in-law) and the sons (Scott Blackstone and Bradley Fox) went together into the great wilderness of northern Quebec, Canada. Three of those six men are now in glory, three remain on earth. They are in their canoe; we are in ours. We paddle a few strokes behind them. They are lost from view, but they are not lost. This is not a gloomy picture, but a glorious portrait of my son "beyond the bend."

In 1506, there was a monument erected to the great discoverer Christopher Columbus. What remains fascinating about the memorial is the lion destroying a motto that had governed the Spanish world for centuries. It was, "Ne Plus Ultra," which means, "No More Beyond." The statue shows the lion tearing way the word, "Ne/No." Columbus had proven in his journeys west that there was indeed, "more beyond!" As John Greenleaf Whittier once wrote, "I know not where His islands lift their fronded palms in air; I only know I cannot drift 'beyond' His love and care!"

As I conclude this book, I pray that you are as convinced as I am in the belief of "beyond the bend, the blue and the borderland." There is no doubt that a "life that is fairer than day" awaits those who believe. I also believe with the great theologian G. Campbell Morgan, "The veil that divided us from the life on the other side seems to grow thinner as our dear ones pass within it!" During these days, especially April 1, 2017 when my son departed, it is a comfort to know that heaven is not as remote as it can sometimes feel. Heaven, on days like that, is just around the corner, just on the other side of the curve, just over the next hill, just "beyond the bend!" This truth is why we cannot drive our stakes to deep, carry too much stuff, or focus too much on today. We might be moving in the morning, just like Scott did. With each departed loved one, we are drawn more and more to over there. Doesn't it make you want to paddle a bit faster, so you can get a glimpse of what is in store?

Conclusion

Account Closed

I AM REMINDED OF a verse from the pen of the Apostle Paul after receiving a morning call from my daughter in California who is attempting to close all Scott's accounts. Paul taught the church, *"So then every one of us shall give account of himself to God"* (Romans 14:12). The passing of a loved one always generates loose ends. I played the role my daughter is playing now, when I took over the affairs of my Uncle Paul in 2008. Uncle Paul taught me a lot about accounting, as his will indicates a certain number of people he wanted to bless after his departure. As I transferred his funds from different banks into one central location, each transaction resulted in "CLOSED" being written over the account. Needless to say, I had to close quite a few accounts, considering Uncle Paul had his money in three states and three different financial institutions. Talking to Marnie and remembering the closing of Uncle Paul's estate, has caused me to ponder how I will close out this accounting of my son's final days on earth.

Everyone always wants more time when they know they have no more time. Everyone thinks of heaven when heaven is the only thing they can think about. Most wait too long before starting to make heavenly deposits in accounts that will never close (Matthew 6:19–21). The great thing about those eternal accounts is they yield high interest rates; you will never have to worry about inflation or bankruptcy, and taxes and fees will never deplete the account. Even if you have but pennies in those heavenly accounts you are richer than the billionaire here. It will be a great relief when we join our loved ones there because we will be able to stop rendering to Caesar the things that are Caesars and we will only be dealing with God and God things. Truly heaven will contain something better in the area of accounts, for the treasures of Heaven far out weight the gold and silver of earth. Maybe these lines from a simple sermon I found in a "Sword of the Lord' magazine will help you understand what I speak of:

"A man asked a few different people the same question, but he got a different answer from each, 'What is Heaven?' I asked a child, 'All joy,' and in her innocence she smiled. I asked the aged, with her care oppressed, all suffering over, 'Oh, Heaven at last is rest.' I asked the artist, who adored his art, 'Heaven is all beauty,' spoke his ruptured heart. I asked the poet with soul afire, 'Tis glory,' and he struck his lyre. I asked the Christian waiting for his release, a halo round him, 'Lo,' he answered, 'Peace': so all may look with hopeful eyes above, tis beauty, glory, joy, rest, peace and love."

How many of us respond like the lady who went to her doctor to find out why she had been feeling so bad, only to find out nothing could be done, and said, "My soul! Has it come to that?" Why do we tarry so long at the medical center, doctors office or cancer clinic, when in the end our lives are in the hands of God? Who is better to see us through the deep waters of cancer than the Almighty? I like the theology of a Scotsman who tried to comfort and encourage a fellow traveller over a creek. The friend began to panic the minute he entered the stream, and the Scotsman said, "Who ever heard of anybody drowning with his head high above water?" A believer is always "safe in the arms of Jesus," no matter the river-crossing, walk along a dangerous precipice or hanging over an abyss. Scott's journey through cancer canyon felt as though we had encountered all three of these. We often forget the lesson of the mountain wanderer who slipped off a cliff, only to save himself by grabbing a small bush. He hung and hung, screaming for help, but no one came. Finally, he realized he would die, and made the decision to let go. When he did drop, he fell but two inches to an overhanging below him. One of the last things I said to Scott before his Saturday morning departure was, "Let go and let God."

In the final accounting of Scott's life, I tried to teach him the theology of the great English pastor Charles Haddon Spurgeon, "That God is too good to be unkind, too wise to make a mistake, and when you cannot trace the hand of God, you can always trust His heart!" We must always remember that the heart of God directs the hand of God. We need not question the hand. Do I still have more unanswered questions than I have answers? Certainly. But, I hope these thoughts of a father, written in the last five weeks of his son's earthly life have convinced you that I believe that what God put Scott through was for His glory and our good (Romans 8:28).

My prayer, as I close this accounting, is that you my reader will recognize that when my son's funeral comes and I speak on the events of the last six months, my congregation will see my genuine confidence that God did know best, and that His plan for my son was worked out according to this divine purpose and perfect providence. Grace is not cheap. Mercy is not without cost. Many times, I have preached on Satan's willingness to pay any price to tempt you away from God. The only way to defeat him is to have no price! Jesus taught us this principle in the wilderness temptation when He had no price, including the glories of the entire world (Matthew 4:1–10). Christ's response was unlike Judas who did have a price (Luke 22:1–6), as well as Demas (II Timothy 4:10), and Ananias (Acts 5:3). Holiness is also not cheap, and being conformed to the image of Christ will cost us everything. This is why Jesus taught His earliest disciples, and they passed it along to us, "So likewise, whosoever he be of you that forsaketh not all that he hath, he cannot be my disciple" (Luke 14:33).

A few days ago, I emailed my version of Scott's obituary to my daughter for her approval. Before it came back to me, Marnie had taken my facts and rewrote them into a beautiful tribute to her brother. She is the real writer of the family! I tell people that writing is my way to deal with my feelings and emotions. Some people eat, others cry, and I write during difficult times. I do not know if this will help anyone else, but it has helped me. During Scott's illness, I officially became a senior citizen and am now drawing Social Security. I will go through this new venture in my life without my son. I would be foolish to want him back, but just maybe I will play a better game, run a better course and fight a better fight knowing who is in the grandstand cheering me on (Hebrew 12:1)!

Obituary

I, Scott Alexander Blackstone, born in Concord, New Hampshire on November 7, 1977, departed this earth on April 1, 2017. Ok, man, that's way too formal for me already. I guess when you die, you're supposed to talk about your life and stuff. So, here's my life in review.

My Dad is a pastor. So, you know what that means. We moved a lot growing up. I lived in four different towns: Concord, New Hampshire; Westfield, Eastport and Ellsworth, Maine. Only one church and town did I ever call home though, Emmanuel Baptist Church in Ellsworth. The people of Emmanuel, that's what made it home.

I loved sports of any kind. Give me a bat, a ball, a club or a fishing pole and I found my sweet spot. In high school, basketball was my thing. I scored 1198 points for Temple Christian Academy (I know the exact number, because my Dad is a statistic junkie. You'll find this out as I continue. Everyone knows I have a horrible memory—thank you ARMY for all the concussions). My first job ended up being on a golf course and gave me a love for the game. No matter where I was, east coast, west coast or in the middle of the desert, I loved swinging a club, even if it was just a makeshift stick.

When I turned twenty-nine, I came home and shocked my parents by saying, "So. . .I enlisted." I joined the United States ARMY and began my adventures travelling from one duty station to the next. During my eight years of active duty, I lived on five ARMY bases and served in three deployments (Fort Knox, Kentucky; Fort Leonard Wood, Missouri; Fort Benning, Georgia; Fort Wainwright, Alaska and Fort Bragg, North Carolina). The ARMY trained me in heavy equipment transportation, which allowed me to run convoys in the Middle East. On my first deployment to Iraq, I participated in 25 missions and drove 25,000 dangerous miles as a gunship driver guarding supply convoys with the 546th, attached to the 82nd Airborne (2007–2008).

The ARMY decided my time in the sandbox needed to continue. So, I deployed again with the 126th to Afghanistan. My training as a Heavy Equipment Transport (HET) driver to the Forward Observation Bases (FOB) scattered around Helmand Province took me on thirteen different combat missions (2010–2011). Those months were the toughest of my life. Four of my closest battle buddies died in IED explosions before my eyes. Till my last breath, I wore a bracelet in honor of Joshua Campbell, Shawn Muhr, Devin Daniels and Colby Richmond. They were gone, but never forgotten.

My Dad and Mom would want me to talk about my eleven medals of commendation and the battle that earned me a purple heart. But, I don't want the recognition. I never did. I did what was asked of me. We all did. People lost a whole lot more than me and should have gotten way more medals than I did. It was an honor to serve. Although when my time was up, I was more than ready to leave active duty and join the ARMY Reserves.

Life as a civilian looked different for me. I took my training from the ARMY and got licensed for a different kind of heavy equipment— construction rigs. I worked for Old Castle Lawn and Garden in Fayetteville, North Carolina, where I played in the dirt with life sized Tonka trucks all day. I bought my first Harley Davison motorcycle and took to the open road. I loved the wind in my face, forgetting everything behind me.

Just when life was gettin' really good, I got sick. I fought the hardest battle of my life, for six months. In the end, the hardest part of dying was saying good-bye to my Mom and Dad. Man, I love them. They have always been there for me, no matter what I put them through. But, I left them in good hands with my sister, Marnie, her man, Josue, and their son Judah, the most amazing little man I know (and now a little lady named Elena). We didn't have enough time together. I wanted to teach Judah to play golf, see the California coast, and find a few more fishing holes with my dad and talk late into the night with my Mom like we always did. But, God had different plans.

I'm enjoying a better place, with people I haven't seen in a long time, like my grandfather (Stacy Meister, 1997, and Wendell Blackstone, 2017). I'm cancer free and living in unspeakable joy with the Lord. I was ready to die, even though I didn't want to. I had so much more life to live. More adventures to experience. More open roads to ride on with my Harley. More golf holes to birdie. I told my sister before I died that I had no regrets. I always said I was "livin' the dream." I meant it, even in the dark days of war and loss and heartache. I loved my life, my friends, and my family. I was a blessed man.

www.ingramcontent.com/pod-product-compliance
Lightning Source LLC
Chambersburg PA
CBHW070821250626
47170CB00006B/2176